THE TREE OF LOVE

It was now the fourth day she had been in the house and Shenda played the piano in the boudoir after attending to the Captain's wounds as she had every day.

She found the piano gave her an enormous amount of pleasure and she really loved composing whatever she was thinking about.

Now the music she was playing was the story of her growing up and of her happiness at being with her parents.

And of the magic she found amongst the flowers in the garden and in the woods.

She played how the squirrels carried their nuts up the trees to hide them and how the goblins would work in the roots as she listened to them by putting her ear against the trunks.

She played to the brilliant stars overhead and to the moon creeping up the sky that had always fascinated her.

She played the tunes all the birds sang in the spring and then her feelings as she first saw the Seine and thought how beautiful it was.

The music of the Seine made her think of Pluck and how the brave little dog had swum to safety after his cruel owner had tried to drown him.

Then she played of her delight when she and Pierre had rescued him and how they had brought him home in triumph!

THE BARBARA CARTLAND PINK COLLECTION

Titles in this series

THE TREE OF LOVE

BARBARA CARTLAND

Barbaracartland.com Ltd

THE BARBARA CARTLAND PINK COLLECTION

Barbara Cartland was the most prolific bestselling author in the history of the world. She was frequently in the Guinness Book of Records for writing more books in a year than any other living author. In fact her most amazing literary feat was when her publishers asked for more Barbara Cartland romances, she doubled her output from 10 books a year to over 20 books a year, when she was 77.

She went on writing continuously at this rate for 20 years and wrote her last book at the age of 97, thus completing 400 books between the ages of 77 and 97.

Her publishers finally could not keep up with this phenomenal output, so at her death she left 160 unpublished manuscripts, something again that no other author has ever achieved.

Now the exciting news is that these 160 original unpublished Barbara Cartland books are already being published and by Barbaracartland.com exclusively on the internet, as the international web is the best possible way of reaching so many Barbara Cartland readers around the world.

The 160 books are published monthly and will be numbered in sequence.

The series is called the Pink Collection as a tribute to Barbara Cartland whose favourite colour was pink and it became very much her trademark over the years.

The Barbara Cartland Pink Collection is published only on the internet. Log on to www.barbaracartland.com to find out how you can purchase the books monthly as they are published, and take out a subscription that will ensure that all subsequent editions are delivered to you by mail order to your home.

NEW

Barbaracartland.com is proud to announce the publication of ten new Audio Books for the first time as CDs. They are favourite Barbara Cartland stories read by well-known actors and actresses and each story extends to 4 or 5 CDs. The Audio Books are as follows:

The Patient Bridegroom	The Passion and the Flower
A Challenge of Hearts	Little White Doves of Love
A Train to Love	The Prince and the Pekinese
The Unbroken Dream	A King in Love
The Cruel Count	A Sign of Love

More Audio Books will be published in the future and the above titles can be purchased by logging on to the website www.barbaracartland.com or please write to the address below.

If you do not have access to a computer, you can write for information about the Barbara Cartland Pink Collection and the Barbara Cartland Audio Books to the following address:

Barbara Cartland.com Ltd., Camfield Place,
Hatfield, Hertfordshire AL9 6JE, United Kingdom.

Telephone: +44 (0)1707 642629
Fax: +44 (0)1707 663041

THE LATE DAME BARBARA CARTLAND

Barbara Cartland who sadly died in May 2000 at the age of nearly 99 was the world's most famous romantic novelist who wrote 723 books in her lifetime with worldwide sales of over 1 billion copies and her books were translated into 36 different languages.

As well as romantic novels, she wrote historical biographies, 6 autobiographies, theatrical plays, books of advice on life, love, vitamins and cookery. She also found time to be a political speaker and television and radio personality.

She wrote her first book at the age of 21 and this was called *Jigsaw*. It became an immediate bestseller and sold 100,000 copies in hardback and was translated into 6 different languages. She wrote continuously throughout her life, writing bestsellers for an astonishing 76 years. Her books have always been immensely popular in the United States, where in 1976 her current books were at numbers 1 & 2 in the B. Dalton bestsellers list, a feat never achieved before or since by any author.

Barbara Cartland became a legend in her own lifetime and will be best remembered for her wonderful romantic novels, so loved by her millions of readers throughout the world.

Her books will always be treasured for their moral message, her pure and innocent heroines, her good looking and dashing heroes and above all her belief that the power of love is more important than anything else in everyone's life.

"As many of you will know I have been an ardent believer of the amazing benefits of natural medicine all my life, but always remember that a combination of nature and love together will cure any malady or illness."

Barbara Cartland

CHAPTER ONE
1815

Shenda brought her stallion into the stables and as there was no groom to be seen she rubbed him down.

Then she patted him affectionately and walked out onto the cobbled yard.

There was still no sign of the groom anywhere and she thought he was doubtless in the kitchen talking to the cook about the funeral.

She walked slowly, not into the house, but through the rhododendrons that led into the garden.

The grass was green and so many flowers were just coming into bloom.

The birds were singing cheerfully overhead, but all Shenda could think about was that this was the end.

The end of her life as she knew it.

The end of her home, the only one she had ever known.

It seemed so incredible that everything could have changed so much since the beginning of the war.

Her mother had died not long before the end of the Peninsular Campaign and she realised that she would have to look after her father, who had never been very strong – he had always relied on his wife for everything.

Nobody could have dreamt that Lady Linbury, who had always been the spirit and inspiration of the whole County, could have died so suddenly.

It was after an exceptionally bitter winter and she had always been weak where her lungs were concerned.

When she caught what was in fact a very bad attack of pneumonia, she refused to take to her bed.

She insisted on continuing to look after her husband and her daughter as she had always done.

When she could no longer move, see or speak, she had reluctantly agreed to rest, but it was too late.

The doctor could do nothing and the nurse they had ordered for her arrived after she had actually passed away.

To Shenda it had seemed quite impossible that her darling Mama was no longer there with her.

Everyone turned to her for help and advice and she had always been an incredible tower of strength not only to Linbury House but also to the estate that had been in the family for generations.

The system was old-fashioned in very many ways, but what did that matter.

As Shenda's brother Johnnie had said to her over and over again,

"I will alter things and bring the estate up-to-date when I take over. But for the moment I am quite content to let Mama do everything she wants."

It was not as if he was able to do much anyway, as being in the Army he could take very little leave.

He had travelled abroad with the first contingent of Wellington's Army on the outbreak of war.

After he had landed in Portugal it was impossible at first to hear from him at all and then occasionally letters came through – yet invariably by the time they arrived they were out of date.

Therefore they had no idea where Johnnie was or, as his father sometimes said bitterly, "if he is alive at all."

Shenda had written to him when their mother died, but it was two months before she received an answer.

When Johnnie learnt of his mother's death, he was, as Shenda expected, terribly upset by the news.

"What will we do without her," he wrote, *"she was always the life and soul of the family, and I cannot imagine how you and Papa will cope now she is no longer there."*

It was exactly what Shenda was thinking herself.

She could only write back to him and tell Johnnie they were doing their best and when he did return he would not be disappointed.

Then the Battle of Waterloo came and the whole of the country was in a wild state of excitement at the victory.

But Johnnie was one of those thousands of English soldiers who would never return.

It was hearing that he had lost his only son, Shenda recognised, that had really killed her father.

Losing her mother had been the blow that changed him into a withdrawn invalid who seldom spoke and only ate when his daughter more or less forced him to do so.

Shenda had always known her father was frail, but then one morning when the servant who called him came hurrying to her room, she knew as she heard his footsteps in the corridor what he had come to tell her.

Now without her father, her mother or Johnnie to guide her, she had to make what she realised was the most important decision of her life.

Actually there was no alternative.

She had to do what her father had told her to do.

She had read the letter he had left for her again and again.

At first she felt that what he had written to her must be part of her imagination and not of reality.

Living as she was in the depths of the Hertfordshire countryside she had always felt out of touch with the world outside her home and its immediate neighbourhood.

There had been no question of her going to London a year ago when she would ordinarily have made her debut in the Season.

One of her very distant relatives had written to say that she fully understood what a sad time it was for her and wondered if she would like to come and stay in London.

She was in mourning and therefore could not attend any of the Society balls, but there were many small parties at which she could be a guest.

Some of her younger cousins whom she had never met would doubtless invite her to visit them.

In the past Shenda had refused because she had her father to look after and anyway she had thought it was not the sort of world she would enjoy.

Now her father had been buried two days ago and there had been no one to mourn at his funeral except their immediate neighbours.

They were mostly older and living quietly without having any young as their sons were serving in the Army of Occupation in France and their daughters were married or so young they were still at school.

Though her father was a Peer, he was not a wealthy man and during the years of the war he and her mother had not been that interested in Social activities in the County.

Shenda gathered that things had been very different when her father and mother had been young. When they first married there had been more kindred spirits living in that part of Hertfordshire than there were now.

She was amused when she was told that the Duke of Wellington, who was then Sir Arthur Wellesley, used to stay at Hatfield House with their neighbours the Marquis and Marchioness of Salisbury.

Shenda had been told that Lady Salisbury had given him a sky-blue frock-coat, the colours of the Hertfordshire Hunt and he had obviously appreciated the gift as he often wore it when he rode to hounds.

The Salisburys had always seemed somewhat aloof from their neighbours in the County, but still they had sent her a letter of condolence when her mother died.

She expected that there would be another one when they learnt of the death of her father.

What her father and mother had told her about the Duke of Wellington was all she knew about him.

Now suddenly, so that it took her breath away even to think about it, he had become very important in her life.

After her father's death she had gone to his writing desk to see what bills were outstanding. To her surprise when she opened the centre drawer, she had seen her name printed in capital letters on a large envelope.

She had stared at it for a moment, thinking she was only seeing it in her imagination.

She recognised her father's handwriting and opened the brown envelope gingerly.

Inside there was one envelope for her – and another one addressed, although it seemed incredible, to *His Grace the Duke of Wellington.*

She opened hers and her father had written,

"My dearest and most precious daughter,

When you read this, which I think will be very soon, I will have joined your mother and your beloved brother in another world.

As I have often felt them near me, I am quite certain they will be there to welcome me and I will not be alone.

But there is no one left to look after you!

This has troubled me night after night when I have lain awake wondering how you will ever be able to care for yourself.

I have finally decided that you must go to France when you have read this letter and give the letter I have enclosed with yours to the Duke of Wellington.

I have pointed out to him that I have given him my one and only son and the well-being of my estate as all our men who used to work for us have joined his Army.

Now the only one I have left is you, Shenda.

I therefore leave you in his care and feel sure that he will not refuse my plea.

If Johnnie had survived to carry on my title and the estate, you would, I know, have been happy. When the war was over, you could have lived the life your mother and I had always planned for you.

As everything has changed and all that is left of this hideous and ghastly war is the peace the Duke can bring to Europe, you surely have a right to share in his victory.

God Bless you, my dearest beloved daughter, and please obey me as I believe that I am doing what both your mother and Johnnie would think is right and just."

Her father had signed it at the bottom of the page.

Shenda read it again, feeling it could not be true.

Also in her envelope was the name and address of a courier in London who would take her to France and there was quite a large sum of money for her expenses.

*

Now she stood in the middle of the garden, looking at the flowers and shrubs that were so familiar and the trees she and Johnnie had climbed when they were children.

She looked beyond to the lake where they had both learnt to swim and fish.

But still she could not believe that she must leave the home that had always been hers –

And all the love that had been poured into it by her beloved family.

As Johnnie was now dead, so was the title and the house and estate would have to be sold because there was not enough income for her to keep them going. Nor would it be possible for her to live there alone.

As her father had said in his letter, the men working on the estate – and many had been with them for years – had all gone to the war.

Many had been killed or wounded and there was no prospect therefore of their ploughing the acres again and making the crops pay as they had done before the war.

Just as they now looked sad and neglected, so did the house itself.

It was almost impossible, even if she could afford it, to have the necessary repairs undertaken.

The winter rain had seeped in through the ceilings, and the tiles had fallen off the roof, and there had been no workmen to replace them or to make sure that there was no further damage in the next tempest.

The last few winters had been rough and very cold and when they had killed her mother, they had destroyed part of the house which was now uninhabitable.

Now whenever she looked at the house, she closed her eyes as she could not bear to see how many windows needed repairing.

The house would one day fall down, or it would be left to the next owner to restore it to its former glory.

At the same time everything in her body rebelled against going abroad.

How could she ever leave the England she loved so much where everything was so familiar?

Yet she knew that her father would think of it as an adventure for her.

When he was a young man he had spent much time exploring the world and had visited many strange countries that seldom appeared in the geography books.

Shenda could remember sitting on a stool at his feet while he told her stories – how he had climbed a mountain in India and how he had travelled to Nepal where few other Europeans had ever been and how he had then explored the great unknown African deserts.

He made it all seem so fascinating, vivid and real to the small child listening to him entranced and it was even better when she could follow his finger on the map.

'If only my Papa was able to come with me now,' she thought, 'it would be exciting, but if I go alone it will be frightening and embarrassing, especially if the Duke has no wish to look after me as Papa has requested.'

She could hardly imagine why at the moment of his victory and now busy organising the Army of Occupation, he should take the slightest notice of her.

Yet, as her father had once said,

"Friendship is what counts ultimately in this world. The friendship of those you meet, if only for a short time, should remain with you in your mind and your heart, never to be forgotten."

She knew her father had felt that about the Duke of Wellington.

He had known him first of all when he was serving in India and they had apparently become friends, although her father was much older.

He had watched the extraordinary rise of the Duke from an unknown and not particularly successful soldier.

And now he was the greatest soldier, the greatest diplomat, and to many beautiful women, the greatest lover.

At the same time it was one thing to admire a man and to recognise him as the greatest conqueror of his time – quite another to be handed over to him as if she were just a book or a piece of Dresden china.

'If he has any sense he will refuse to have anything to do with me,' thought Shenda. 'If I was sensible, I would take the money Papa has left for me and spend it finding a small cottage and somewhere to work.'

However, she was not certain what that work could be or what she might be capable of doing.

With no prospect in sight for the future and no one to protect her as her parents had done, she would have to find a place where people were kind and understanding.

Equally she was well aware that her mother would be shocked at the idea of her being unchaperoned.

Even if she was to live in a small cottage in a small village, people would know she was alone and consider it imprudent and actually improper.

'*I suppose I shall have to go to France,*' she sighed.

Then her whole being flowed out to the garden – to the flowers she loved and always bloomed year after year just for her – and above all to her many memories.

There had once been white pigeons on the lawn and a golden fountain that she had loved as a child.

What was more hurtful than anything was to have to leave her beautiful stallion.

She had ridden Samson every day since her father had given him to her on her sixteenth birthday.

If Samson was permitted to do so, he would follow her unbridled and un-led anywhere she went.

She could not bear to actually give him away and so she had asked a farmer who lived near the village if he would keep Samson for her and he had promised to do so.

"I've a grandson who'll be that 'appy to ride 'im," he said. "I 'opes 'e'll grow up to be as good a rider as you be, Miss Linbury, and I knows 'e'll come to no 'arm on that there 'orse."

He refused to take any of Shenda's money although she had offered some to him.

"You be doin' I a favour and saving I from 'avin' to buy me grandson a donkey," the farmer continued. "You keep all your money in your pocket, Miss Linbury. You'll find it goes away quick enough if you goes amongst 'em Frenchies."

Shenda had told the farmer she was going to France and that was why she was leaving her stallion with him.

He had guessed, although he did not say so, that she was going to visit the grave of her brother.

It was indeed something she intended to do if it was at all possible, but she had no idea where he was buried or even if the Duke of Wellington would know where.

It was agonising to say goodbye to the garden and the lake where she had learnt to swim and where she had once been pushed in by her boisterous brother.

Her mother had been angry, but her father laughed.

"The children are growing up," he counselled, "and they will have to look after themselves in the future. It is going to be a different world, Elizabeth, from the one we enjoyed when we were first married."

That was indeed true, Shenda reflected.

The war had changed everything.

Nothing would be the same as it had once been.

She went into the house and climbed wearily up the stairs to her bedroom.

One of the local women came from the village each morning to clean the kitchen and cooked Shenda's meal at midday.

After her father's death she just cooked something simple for herself at night, although sometimes she was too lazy or too tired to bother.

Now she could hear Mrs. Smithson moving about in the kitchen, but she had no wish to talk to her.

She realised that soon they would all be wanting to say goodbye to her, and it would be impossible for them to do so without someone crying and they would tell her over and over again how much they would miss her.

What she had to do now was to pack all the things she would need.

Some of her clothes, which she decided she would not wear again, she would give away to the villagers. She had already given away a lot of her mother's clothes, but had kept the best for herself.

She thought she would take these with her – they were rather out of date but still serviceable.

As she had no idea what she would do in France, it could be a mistake to be overdressed.

Her clothes were simple and in good taste and she was well aware that if nothing else she certainly looked a lady in them.

However, she was sure that the Duke, who had all the beautiful women of Europe around him, would find her dull and unattractive.

There were endless rumours even in the depths of the countryside that he was enjoying himself with a great number of lovely women.

Even before her mother had died there was always someone who had a story about the Duke which they felt compelled to tell her.

Lady Charlotte Bentinck, daughter of the third Earl of Portland, was one of the first names that Shenda, now in the schoolroom, heard mentioned in connection with the Duke of Wellington, then Sir Arthur Wellesley.

She had not really listened and yet she remembered that the woman had told her that Arthur Wellesley had met Lady Charlotte in London when he returned from India.

The woman had claimed it was quite clear that they were lovers.

She had lowered her voice so that Shenda did not hear the last word and it was only later that she understood what she had actually said.

Now she remembered that later when she was a bit older, she had overheard another conversation.

Lady Charlotte's home in the *Hôtel d'Angleterre* in Brussels was the focal point of all the news, military and Social.

Also and it had been emphasised as extraordinary, Lady Charlotte gave a party every evening for the principal visitors then in Brussels, including the Duke of Wellington.

Shenda asked herself now, if he had been so busy with such beautiful women, was it likely that he would be willing to have her thrust upon him?

At the same time there was nothing else she could do but to obey her father's last request.

Therefore she continued to pack up her clothes and wondering where they and she would eventually end up.

*

It was just two days later when she finally took the plunge and travelled to London.

She had intended to go there by post chaise, which obviously would have been expensive.

But the son of one of the farmers had said he was going to London with a large consignment of produce. He intended to sell it at Smithfield Market and would welcome her company on the journey.

It was hardly the right way, Shenda mused, that her mother and father would have envisaged her starting off on a journey that was to end with the Duke of Wellington.

Equally it would be ridiculous to travel alone and to spend so much money on doing so.

So she had therefore thanked the young man and accepted his offer and she had sat beside him in his cart.

Actually it was far more comfortable than she had expected and the two horses drawing the cart were spirited and far quicker than the usual farm animals.

They reached London in under three hours which Shenda thought was exceptional.

The young farmer deposited her with her luggage at the office where she could find the courier her father had instructed her to use.

He turned out to be an elderly but well-spoken man, who remembered her father well and was only too willing to accompany her to France.

"I need to find the Duke of Wellington," she told him, "but I am not very certain whether he will be in Paris, where I understand he has a house in the *Champs Élysées*, or with the Army of Occupation at Cambrai."

For a moment the courier looked non-plussed and then he suggested,

"I have an idea, Miss Linbury, that one of our men, who has recently been to France might know. If you let me speak to him, I am sure he will have the latest news of His Grace's movements."

He left Shenda sitting in the low-ceilinged entrance to the office.

People kept coming and going past her and it took her a little time to realise that this must be where a number of people made their reservations to travel.

The courier came back to say,

"I am led to understand that His Grace the Duke of Wellington is, at the moment, at his house in the *Champs Élysées*, and there is no reason at all, Miss Linbury, why we cannot reach Dover this evening in time to board a ferry to carry us to Ostend."

This, Shenda thought with a little quiver of delight, was where the adventure really started.

She had adored travelling with her father although it had only been very occasionally and she had also always enjoyed travelling in her mind.

Now it was a reality.

She desperately wanted her father with her to make sure she missed nothing of the trip.

It took quite a long time as the road was very rough and they did not reach Dover until it was nearly midnight.

Although the road was being repaired in a number of places, the courier pointed out that there was a shortage of men to do the work owing to the war.

It was an excuse she had heard thousands of times already and she was very certain that it was something she would hear a thousand times more in the future.

The courier took her to a comfortable hotel which

was not expensive, and the guests, who never stayed more than a night or two, were not particularly interesting.

To Shenda's surprise she slept peacefully.

*

The following day they set off soon after dawn on the first ferry to cross the English Channel.

It was overcrowded and the service was practically non-existent, but as Shenda had somewhere to sit she did not worry. She was only too thankful and too excited when she stepped out onto French soil.

She left the courier to fight for seats on the coach for Paris which would leave as soon as it was full.

The carriage was quick and the service where they changed horses was swift.

They could, the courier informed her, reach Paris in twelve hours, but it was always very uncertain what might happen en route – not surprisingly they were delayed first by a loose wheel and then one of the horses went lame.

It was late in the afternoon when they finally drove into the Capital City that Shenda had heard so much about.

She was so excited at seeing the tall houses and the narrow alleys crowded with people moving around.

After Napoleon's last fling and his final defeat at Waterloo, the International Peace Conference had opened in July 1815 in Vienna.

The Duke of Wellington and Viscount Castlereagh were the British delegates and Britain's colours were flying high on the Continent.

It was undoubtedly Wellington's hour and he could say, as he had declared before the Battle of Talavera, "the ball is at my foot and I do hope I shall have the strength to give it a good kick!"

But on this occasion the hour was to have its trials.

Art was the first great French grievance.

It seemed correct to the Allies that the art treasures seized by victorious French Armies should, after they had been finally defeated, be returned to their rightful owners.

The Duke's policy was deliberately temperate and he was determined not to hurt the feelings of Louis XVIII, the restored King of France.

He did not, for one instance, go to the extreme of demanding the Bayeux Tapestries for England, nor did he encourage British enterprise at the expense of the French.

In fact, when one of his *aides-de-camp* at Waterloo bought the field of Agincourt and began prodding amongst the French bones, the Duke was asked to intervene.

He commented sardonically later,

"I gave Woodford a hint to dig no more."

However despite the Duke's moderation it took two months of bitter argument for the French Government to agree to any restitution of art treasures.

Shenda had read in the papers about the tremendous row there had been at the Louvre.

British soldiers had given the Dutch permission to remove everything they claimed as theirs although Parisian workmen refused to unhook the Italian pictures.

When they had carried out the *Venus di Medici* feet first, they were accosted by outraged onlookers and Shenda had read that so much fuss was created that the Duke had to arrange the removal of the Parisians' favourite trophies at night, including the four bronze horses from St. Mark's Basilica in Venice.

They had been erected by Napoleon on a triumphal arch in the *Place du Carrousel.*

The Venetians had wept and booed as their beloved

Byzantine horses were brought down one by one in chains from the façade of St. Mark's.

Therefore to spare French feelings and to avoid a similar disturbance, Wellington ordered the bronze horses to be moved at night.

He hoped that the French would sleep whilst they were taken away and under only just a few Officers twenty civilians with their tools started to work.

Suddenly there was a loud noise.

The National Guard then burst right into the *Place du Carrousel*, followed by a raging mob and stopped them.

The following morning the Duke arrived, expecting to find the work completed and in a rage he ordered three thousand Austrians to seal off the *Place du Carrousel*.

Each horse was finally brought down to uproarious cheering while the howling mob was kept outside.

It had amused Shenda to read all this in the London *Morning Post*.

She was wondering whether she would see endless empty spaces everywhere in Paris from which the countries overrun by Napoleon had recovered their treasures.

When Shenda and the courier had been set down after the long journey from Ostend, they took an ordinary fiacre and the courier instructed the driver to take them to the *Champs Élysées*.

It was thrilling for Shenda to be driven through the *Place de la Concorde* and she remembered clearly how the fearsome guillotine had once stood there with the King of France behaving with great bravery before the mob cut off his head.

The thought of it made her shudder, but she could not help finding the *Place de la Concorde* itself was even lovelier than she thought it would be.

The *Champs Élysées* was wide and impressive and only then did she forget her interest in everything the Duke had been doing to restore the treasures of Europe.

Now she realised she had to meet him in person!

Suddenly she wished that she could turn the fiacre round and somehow return to England.

At least there she could be herself and she would be among people who would sympathise with all that she was feeling because they too had suffered from the war.

The fiacre now rumbled to a standstill outside an extremely impressive house. It had iron gates admitting to a beautiful and well-cultivated garden.

"We have arrived at our destination, Miss Linbury," the courier announced.

"I am most grateful to you for looking after me so well," Shenda managed to say.

She paid him out of the money her father had left for her and added a large tip.

The driver of the fiacre waited for the gates to open and they drove in as servants appeared at the front door.

Shenda alighted and her luggage was taken down from the front of the fiacre.

It was then that she wondered, if the Duke refused to accept her, what she should do and where she should go.

Already the courier was saying his farewells as she thanked him again for his courtesy and he drove away.

She suddenly realised that she did not know where to find him to take her home if needs be.

A major-domo was waiting at her side and with an effort Shenda forced herself to speak to him in French,

"I have come to see – His Grace the Duke."

"Please come this way, mademoiselle."

The major-domo led her along a lengthy passage and into an elegantly furnished reception room.

She guessed that it was where those who wanted an audience with the Duke waited until he was ready for them.

The door was closed and she was alone.

She asked herself again frantically if it had been a stupid idea to come –

Supposing the Duke refused to see her.

Supposing he sent her away without even reading her father's letter.

Where could she go and what could she do?

It all passed through her mind almost as clearly as if someone was saying it all aloud.

Then the door opened and a young man in uniform who was obviously an equerry entered the room.

He looked at Shenda with surprise and as he walked towards her, she rose to her feet.

"I have come to see the Duke of Wellington with a letter for him from my father, the late Lord Linbury."

The equerry bowed.

"His Grace is rather busy at the moment," he said, "but I am sure he will be delighted to see you as soon as he is free."

Shenda gave a little sigh of relief before the equerry asked her,

"Have you just come from London?"

"Yes, and it was a somewhat difficult journey, but actually we were quicker than I expected."

"Is this your first visit to Paris?"

"Yes, but, of course, I have read about it and heard so much about the City that I almost feel I have been here."

The equerry laughed.

"We felt the same at first, but I have now been here so long I am beginning to forget London and all the people I knew there."

He was, Shenda recognised, making her feel at ease and at the same time it was somewhat comforting not to be turned away immediately.

She also realised to her surprise that he was looking at her with an expression in his eyes she had not expected.

She could not think of anything further to say and then he remarked,

"There is so much I want to hear about London and about England if it comes to that. I do hope I will have a chance to talk to you after you have seen His Grace."

"That would certainly make me feel more at home than I am feeling at the moment," she replied nervously.

The equerry smiled at her.

"Everyone is frightened before they meet the Duke, but I assure you that when you know him, he has a charm which puts even the most aggressive foreigner at his ease."

He had a twinkle in his eye and Shenda laughed as he walked towards the door.

"I will go and see if the last caller has gone and do not worry, I am quite certain His Grace will be delighted to meet you. You are English, and what can be more pleasant when one is so far from home than to meet someone who speaks the same language from the country we belong to?"

He was gone before Shenda could think of a reply.

She told herself he was certainly the kindest young man she could hope to meet.

'He knew that I was apprehensive,' she reflected, 'and now the Duke of Wellington does not seem half as intimidating as he did before I came here!'

CHAPTER TWO

The Duke's guest rose to his feet saying,

"I cannot thank Your Grace enough for your help, and, of course, your inspiration. I know no one ever leaves you without saying the same thing."

The Duke of Wellington smiled.

"I am always delighted to hear it again."

His guest, who was the newly arrived Ambassador of one of the smaller countries represented in Paris, walked to the door, followed by his wife who had scarcely spoken since they arrived.

She was, however, exceedingly attractive with, the Duke speculated, Russian blood in her.

As he bent over her hand in Parisian fashion, he felt her fingers twitch beneath his.

He rang the bell, an equerry then opened the door and the Ambassador walked out of the room.

Before the door closed his wife came running back saying as she did so,

"I have left my handbag behind!"

It was on the chair where she had been sitting and she picked it up.

Then as she glanced over her shoulder to make sure that neither her husband nor the equerry were to be seen, she moved close to the Duke and whispered,

"Come and see me tomorrow at five o'clock. I will be alone."

His eyes glinted as he looked down at her and then she stood on tiptoe and kissed him on the cheek.

Before he could say anything or move, she had run across the room and disappeared out of the door.

The Duke gave a little laugh.

It was something that often happened to him, but he never failed to find it surprising.

Nevertheless as she was very pretty, he thought he would definitely call on her tomorrow afternoon.

He walked slowly to the window and stood taking in the sun-kissed air before he rang the bell again.

He was thinking, as he had so often done before, of the extraordinary way he had moved up in the world.

What had happened became ever more astounding to him every day.

He found himself thinking of Ireland.

As a penniless First Lieutenant in a Foot Regiment he had been no match for Kitty, the girl he had first wanted to marry in the spring of 1793.

In those days the girls had little choice in who they married.

Kitty's father, Lord Longford, turned him down and he had done so not once but twice.

He was promoted to the rank of Captain in the 18th Light Dragoons then to Major and finally to a Lieutenant-Colonel in the 33rd Foot.

Yet he was still not rated important enough by the relatives of the pretty Irish girl he believed he loved.

He had had a sad childhood, his mother finding him gauche and unattractive and as he often said of himself, "I was a shy reserved boy."

Looking out of the window the Duke thought how fantastic his life was now.

Everything had changed when he left Portsmouth bound for India at the age of twenty-seven.

He could see himself now standing on the deck of the *S.S. Rockingham* with high hopes.

Nine years later he returned home still a bachelor, but with an experience of women that was to remain with him all his life.

He went out as the Honourable Arthur Wellesley, but left as Sir Arthur Wellesley K.B., the victor of Assaye and half-a-dozen other hard fought battles.

He also left behind him many attractive, young but married women who wept when they bid him farewell.

He was considered exceedingly handsome despite a long pale face and a markedly aquiline nose.

But his clear blue eyes were as compelling as his personality.

The ladies, who had found him irresistible in India, were always married and when they encountered him their husbands were soldiering in another part of the country.

Looking back, the Duke knew he had never actually lost his heart and yet he had certainly found the glamorous and elegant ladies of Calcutta intriguing.

The Regimental Mess proved a place for meeting that often led to the excitement of a new *affaire-de-coeur.*

There would be many delicious wines starting with champagne, superb food followed by horseplay and by the next morning a hangover.

His brother, Richard, arrived in India in 1798 as the Governor General and this gave Arthur more standing than he had already.

Richard was talked of as living, not like a Lord, but like a King Emperor while Arthur found himself even more pursued than before by the deserted wives of busy soldiers.

When he left India he was in fact better experienced in such matters than any of his contemporaries.

Kitty's family who had turned him down as just not good enough for their sister now communicated with him.

They informed him that as she had waited for him all this time, he would now be accepted as her suitor.

Although he had not seen her for years, he decided in April to visit Ireland and marry his little Irish beauty.

His clergyman brother Gerald was to marry them and the wedding ceremony took place in the residence of the Longfords on the 16th April 1806.

If he had altered while he was away – so had Kitty.

"She has grown ugly, by Jove!" he muttered to his brother before the ceremony took place.

He was thirty-seven years old and she was thirty-four and thinking back, the Duke remembered it had been a very unsatisfying relationship.

He had enjoyed a fiery love affair with the famous *courtesan*, Harriette Wilson, the previous year and it was clearly impossible for Kitty, an aging virgin, nervous, shy, timid and exceedingly thin, to arouse him in the same way that Harriette had done.

The Duke turned away from the window.

He did not want to remember how disappointing his marriage had been.

If he had used common sense he would not, after so many years of being told he was not good enough for Lord Longford's daughter, have gone ahead and married her.

Now he harboured no wish to think further of what had happened or how much he had enjoyed himself before his marriage.

He rang the bell rather more sharply than usual and one of his equerries immediately opened the door.

"Who else is here to see me?"

"It's a Miss Linbury, Your Grace."

"Bring her in."

He was wondering why he should recall the name – he was sure that he had known no woman called Linbury.

Then as Shenda came into the room, his remarkable memory made him exclaim even before she reached him,

"Your name is Linbury! Any relation to the Lord Linbury who I well remember meeting several times when I stayed with the Salisburys?"

Shenda smiled.

"Yes, of course. My father went to quite a number of their parties and told me he had often met you there."

"Then I am delighted to see you – and interested to learn why you are in Paris."

Shenda held out the letter from her father.

"My father is dead," she replied, "and he wrote this letter to you before he died."

"*Dead*! I am very sorry to hear it."

"He had not been well for some considerable time – but he forced himself to write – this letter."

Her voice trembled as she uttered the last word.

He gave her a quick glance before sitting down at his desk indicating a comfortable chair for Shenda.

She sank into it.

Then the Duke read the letter and as he did so, he was remembering how much he had liked Lord Linbury.

They had met in India as well as at Hatfield House, and he found more amusement there than anywhere else he was invited and it became a second home for him – in fact the type of home he would have liked for himself.

The Great Hall, the minstrel gallery, the library, the lake, the maze in the Park all delighted him.

He had been at Hatfield House when his only son was born and later Lady Salisbury accompanied by her two daughters visited Kitty in Ireland to see the baby.

At the same time inviting the Duke once again to stay with them for the fox-hunting.

It all now flashed through his mind and he recalled the first time he had met Lord Linbury as a fellow guest.

They had talked together when dinner was over and he had been most impressed by everything the older man had to say.

They had become real friends and the Duke looked forward to meeting him again whenever he visited Hatfield House.

As he read the letter Lord Linbury had inscribed to him, he could hardly believe that what he was reading was true and yet he could understand the many difficulties that had faced the dying man.

The greatest of them being the future of his dearest daughter.

He now addressed Shenda,

"I am very sorry to hear that your father is dead and that your brother was killed at Waterloo."

"They both admired you very much, Your Grace."

"I am flattered, but equally I am wondering what I can do about you."

"I know it is really too much to ask, and I do feel embarrassed at coming here, but I did not really know what else I could do."

"What about your relatives?"

"It sounds extraordinary, Your Grace, but actually they do not exist. There are perhaps one or two old cousins

26

who I have not seen for years. But I am quite certain they would have no wish to have me to live with them even if they could afford it."

The Duke looked down at the letter again.

"I presume," he quizzed, "your father had very little to leave you."

"Only the old house, which is falling down and the estate which has not been properly cultivated for years, and my stallion that I have left with a farmer who I know will look after him."

The Duke did not speak.

He was thinking that he had been left with a huge number of problems and difficulties by practically every country now represented in Paris, besides, of course, by the Parisians themselves.

But he had never yet had a young woman without a penny in the world placed in his care.

He was puzzled as to what he could say and do.

What made it even more complicated was that at present he was deeply engaged in an *affaire-de-coeur* with the famous opera singer Madame Guiseppina Grassini.

It was one of his strangest and in many ways his most outrageous affair.

Madame Grassini had been Napoleon Bonaparte's mistress at one time and her voluptuous charms, her lovely contralto voice and her obvious expertise in singing great music made her irresistible to any man.

She spoke a mixture of Italian, French and English and wore a multi-coloured style of dress that had a 'gypsy' look about it.

She had amassed a large fortune from the gifts she demanded and received from her many lovers.

She was most talkative, impulsive and at the same time exceedingly beautiful.

Their first meeting was when she sang at a banquet the Duke had held in Paris for the Czar of Russia.

The Duke had been entranced by her performance and had gone further and been entranced by her as well.

He thought that of all his many love affairs this was the most fiery and the most satisfying.

Because he was infatuated with her he had thought out an idea of making her *The Queen of the Evening* and she became the first singer to be admitted to Society.

At the party the Duke gave for the Czar he seated her on a sofa on a platform in the ballroom, never left her side and then he took her into supper in front of everyone.

It was therefore not surprising that a great number of the titled English ladies present considered it an insult to them and their Social status.

But the Duke was quite oblivious and did not listen to any rebukes nor did they trouble him in the slightest.

She had now been his mistress for nearly a year, but at the back of his mind he had a strong feeling that their love affair was coming to an end.

At the same time it was impossible for him to invite this young innocent girl in front of him to stay in his house even if he provided her with a chaperone.

He thought that the one person he might just ask for help was Madame de Staël.

He had been fascinated by this brilliant woman of letters and he saw her practically every day in Paris.

Her wit and wisdom were always irresistible and she entertained the intellectuals of the day in her home.

However, he was quite certain she would not want to be hampered with a young girl.

'What the devil can I do?' the Duke asked himself as he saw Shenda watching him with worried eyes.

"This is a somewhat difficult situation for you," he began, "and also, as it so happens, for *me*."

"I was certain that was what you would feel, Your Grace, but perhaps if I could stay somewhere respectable, there would be some useful work I could undertake."

The Duke smiled.

"And what do you think that could be?"

Shenda made a helpless gesture with her hands.

"I have done such a lot at home, including nursing my parents, but I cannot think of any special talent I have like dancing or singing that could earn money."

The Duke thought that this was certainly true as at present Paris was filled with many artistes of the greatest talent and all of them anxious to gain his approval and that of the many foreign diplomats in the City –

He was thinking of all the people he knew and was wondering if any of them would be likely to oblige him.

He recognised that the most charming of his female acquaintances were all besotted with him and they would therefore not be prepared to accept an exceedingly pretty young English girl as their guest.

Alternatively if she was found staying in his house, it would undoubtedly ruin her reputation.

Because Shenda was aware that he was finding her a difficulty, she suggested,

"Perhaps, Your Grace, I should stay – in some quiet lodging house whilst you consider – my father's request."

The Duke did not have to look at her.

He realised that with her young attractive face and exquisite pink and white skin, every Frenchman she came across would pursue her and inevitably frighten her.

"I was just thinking," he said, trying to reassure her, "that it should not be difficult to find somewhere for you to stay and something interesting for you to do.

"Paris at present is filled with people from every European country who have all suffered under Napoleon. I will, I feel sure, find you something you will enjoy doing. Equally you must stay with someone I can trust to take care of you."

"You are so kind – and it is wonderful of you not to send me away at once," Shenda enthused, "but I don't want to be an encumbrance on you in any way."

"We have to think about this in a practical manner. First, as you have been travelling, I am sure that you would like something to eat and drink."

"That is most thoughtful of you, Your Grace."

She was really too agitated to want anything.

But she knew that the Duke was taking his time to mull over the problem she had brought to him.

He rang the bell and when the equerry appeared, he told him,

"Miss Linbury is tired after travelling all day and I suggest that she has what the chef will undoubtedly call an 'English tea' in the salon."

The equerry smiled.

"I will order it at once, Your Grace."

"Now tell me a bit more about yourself," the Duke asked Shenda, "and why everything has gone so wrong on your estate."

"I think everything started to go wrong after Mama died. Papa was too upset after her death and then too ill to cope with the difficulties the war brought to us all."

The Duke sighed.

"*The war*! It is always the war. But now at last I am determined that we will have peace. To make sure of it, as you have doubtless heard, we are imposing an Army of Occupation on France, although it might be difficult to keep the men under control when there is no fighting."

"I have read about it in the newspapers."

"I will, of course, be doing a lot of entertaining, but it would not be proper for you to stay as my guest in this house."

He did not add, although he thought it, that it was going to be somewhat difficult to be rid of the attractive Madame Grassini.

He was being honest with himself and he knew that Madame Grassini was well aware that he was looking with more interest at the other women who approached him.

Nothing was said and yet she would already realise instinctively that he was not so completely bemused by her as he had been at the beginning of their affair.

She still thrilled him and because he knew he meant a great deal to her, it was going to be hard to break it off.

He had never been able to disappear at the end of his affairs without tears and broken hearts, although quite a number of his mistresses remained close friends.

It was impossible for the Duke not to think of Lady Georgiana Lennox, whom he had met in 1806 on his return from India. He wrote to her every week when they were not together.

She was exactly the sort of woman he could trust to love him for ever and yet she never reproached him.

Only this May she had ridden with him to a Review of the Brunswick Troops and it had rained heavily and she had returned to Paris wearing a soldier's greatcoat.

The Duke had presented Georgiana with a portrait of himself – an original miniature by a Belgian artist.

She had come to Paris and he knew he would have to spend a great deal of time with her.

As she loved him so much, she had delayed getting married and she was still refusing offer after offer simply because of her adoration for him.

As he ruminated, the Duke found this new problem more and more difficult.

How could he protect this young girl, while at the same time not neglecting women like Georgiana who loved him to distraction?

There were four Parisian theatres where the Duke had his own box every night – they were the *Grand Opera*, *Le Francais*, *le Fédeau* and *des Variétés*.

It had been arranged that the Duke was to attend the *Grand Opera* tonight and he wondered whether he should take Shenda with him.

Then he guessed that it would be a mistake.

Everyone there would be quite certain that she was his latest *affaire-de-coeur*!

That in itself would prejudice her relationship with the more particular hostesses in Paris and he had suffered so often from jealousy amongst his admirers.

The British Government had recently paid the sum of eight hundred thousand francs for a new Embassy that bordered on the Champs Élysées.

He supposed that Shenda might stay there, but the Embassy was not yet complete and he was not sure who he could trust to chaperone her.

'It's such an impossible situation,' he told himself angrily.

Then he realised Shenda was looking at him with a concerned expression in her eyes.

"If I am a nuisance, Your Grace, when you are so wonderful and have done such marvels for England, I must go home. I am afraid very stupidly I let my courier leave without telling me where I can find him in Paris."

"No! No, of course not," the Duke said hurriedly. "Your father has sent you to me and because I had a great affection for him I must respect his wishes. It is just taking me a little time to reflect on where you would be happiest and what you would find most interesting to do."

"Maybe there is a hospital where I can work. Then I will not have to trouble you with my accommodation."

He stared at her and then suddenly he had an idea.

It came to him, he thought, almost as if it was a gift from God at a moment when he most needed it.

Quite the most remarkable and exceptional Officer under his command at the Battle of Waterloo had been the Marquis of Kenworth.

The Duke had met him in London, when he was a young man of twenty-eight, and he had stayed at Hatfield House when he too had been a guest of the Salisburys.

A tall handsome young man, he had been pursued by ambitious mothers for their daughters – and because he was so good-looking by a number of married ladies.

The Duke had spoken to him on various occasions and the Marquis told him that he had a very large estate in the country to look after, together with an ancestral home that had been in his family for many generations.

He decided against joining the smarter Regiments already on active service on the Continent and instead he had become an Officer in the Household Brigade, which for the moment was posted in England.

"When you feel like going to war, Ivan," the Duke had said, "I will of course welcome you with open arms."

The Marquis, who had only just come into the title, smiled at him.

"You are most gracious, sir, and I will not forget your generosity."

He had not said anything more and the Duke had not thought of him again.

Then just before the Battle of Waterloo, when he was short of men and aware that Napoleon had collected a larger Army than his, the Marquis turned up in Brussels.

One look at him told the Duke that he was worried about something.

"It is delightful to see you again, Ivan," he had said holding out his hand.

The Marquis however waited till the door was shut behind him and then he muttered,

"I have arrived here incognito, sir, and my name is Worth. Just plain Mr. Ivan Worth with no title."

The Duke had stared at him in astonishment, before enquiring,

"Why? What has happened?"

"I have no wish to talk about it, but you promised me if I needed help you would give it to me. Well now I am begging you on my knees to keep your promise."

"Of course I will, Ivan, sit down and tell me what has happened and why you are now incognito."

"I have left England because I am disgusted with the behaviour of certain people there," Ivan said slowly. "I wish to fight under you, but not using my own name."

The Duke found all this somewhat perplexing.

However, he was used to strange proposals –

"Very well, tell me what you want and I will try to make it possible."

"I wish to be under your command in your Army," he replied, "and I will accept the rank of Lieutenant so that I am just a junior Officer and no more."

"Very well. If that is your wish, I will give you that rank, but it seems rather strange that as you are already a Captain in the Household Brigade, you should want to go down the ladder rather than up it!"

"I have disappeared from England, sir, for reasons that would not particularly interest you, but have upset and disgusted me. My only request now is that you accept me in your Army and allow me to fight with all my strength and might against Napoleon Bonaparte."

The Duke thought it sounded rather like a drama on the stage, but he was not prepared to argue.

He was far too busy at that very moment to think of anything but the battle that lay ahead, and at the same time an extra Officer was always welcome when he was quite convinced that Napoleon's Army was larger than his own.

He sent Ivan to a Cavalry Regiment and was glad to learn that he had brought his uniform with him, as well as his own batman who would count as another soldier for the forthcoming battle.

Lieutenant Ivan Worth had indeed proved himself an outstanding Officer in a way the Duke had not actually expected. He had managed to hold off a French attack on a key position with the French retreating having lost at least double the number of casualties as the English.

The Duke had been told how Ivan had encouraged the troops under him and they managed to drive off another French attack by making it appear they were much stronger than they actually were.

It was, however, unfortunate that at the very hour of victory Lieutenant Ivan Worth had been badly wounded in the shoulder by a bullet fired by a sniper.

He had been carried unconscious and bleeding from the battle front.

The Duke felt rather responsible for him and knew that he could well afford it, so he had not left him with the other wounded when he travelled to Paris.

He had taken Ivan Worth, now raised to the rank of Captain, with him and settled him in a comfortable house in the *Faubourg St. Honoré* in one of the smartest and most expensive parts of Paris.

The house belonged to a French Vicomte, who was sheltering in the South of France from the ravages of war and it was therefore unoccupied.

The Duke had given orders that Captain Worth was to be installed there and had arranged that nurses should be provided for him and no expense spared.

The Duke's orders were carried out to the letter and Ivan was attempting to regain his strength.

When the Duke had called on him two days ago he was told that the doctors were pleased with his progress, although he would doubtless have to remain convalescent for quite some time yet.

"The only difficulty, Your Grace," his batman told the Duke, "is that the Captain 'as taken a big dislike to the nurses provided and keeps dismissin' them."

The Duke had looked at the man in surprise.

"Why should he do that, Higgins?"

The batman had looked over his shoulder almost as if he felt someone was listening, before replying,

"His Lordship – I means the Captain – 'ad a real unfortunate experience afore he left London."

The Duke raised his eyebrows.

"With a lady?"

The man nodded.

"He'd be ever so angry, Your Grace, if he knew I'd told you. It was someone who he were a-'opin' to marry, but they quarrelled."

The Duke was now beginning to realise why Ivan had come to him and wished to fight in the war.

"Tell me more, Higgins." he demanded.

"As you can imagine, Your Grace, I weren't told much meself. But I knows there were a terrible row 'tween him and Lady Helen Oswald. When 'er walked out of the 'ouse, I packs up and we comes to you."

The Duke had suspected that the reason for Ivan's sudden appearance had something to do with a woman.

'Who else,' he had asked himself, 'could cause so much havoc to a sensible young man?'

"What I really thinks," continued Higgins, "is that 'is Lordship now 'ates all women. He took a big dislike to those what were bandagin' him. Two of them tells me they won't come again whatever the doctors might say!"

It now occurred to the Duke that here was indeed a respectable house where Shenda could stay.

If she was there as a nurse, she would not require a chaperone.

There would certainly be no necessity for one when her patient was too ill to think of love and apparently had a personal dislike of the female sex anyway.

Shenda was sitting upright looking at the Duke with nervous eyes.

He smiled at her.

"It is all right, Miss Linbury, I have solved your problem and I hope that you will find the work I am giving you will be interesting."

"What is it, Your Grace?"

"I want you to nurse a young Officer who has been seriously wounded and who is in a very comfortable house I found for him in the *Faubourg St. Honoré*."

"Do you want me to take care of him?"

"But, of course. He needs a nurse and, as you say you have nursed your father and mother, I am sure you will find no difficulty in carrying out what the doctors require."

Shenda gave a sigh of relief.

"Thank you, thank you so very much, Your Grace, I knew you would not fail to help me, and, of course, I will feel it an honour and a great privilege to help anyone who has fought so bravely at Waterloo."

"I am here if you need me," the Duke said. "In the meantime I will take you there and I am sure you will be very comfortable."

"Thank you, thank you," Shenda repeated. "I think you must be the most marvellous man in the world as you seem to solve everyone's problems. The newspapers have been full of praise for you and I will add to their tributes by saying that I too have found you to be very wonderful."

The Duke smiled.

He was thinking of how the Czar had said to him when Napoleon had reappeared in France from Elba,

"It is up to you to save the world once again – "

It was what he had tried to do and, with God's help, he had been victorious at Waterloo.

But now, as if the cap had been set on him, he was obliged to solve the problems of almost everyone he came into contact with.

'I have done it once again,' he murmured to himself as he rose to his feet.

CHAPTER THREE

The Duke drove from the *Champs Élysées* into the *Place de la Concorde* with Shenda sitting beside him.

"Now I must explain to you," he began, "all about your patient."

Shenda turned to him and became attentive.

"I am led to believe," the Duke said slowly as if he was considering every word, "that Captain Ivan Worth was deeply upset by a woman before he was wounded in battle. He is therefore, I understand, somewhat difficult with his nurses – and he may not be too pleased to see you."

"I expect that is due to his wounds, Your Grace, I know my mother told me about women who hated their husbands anywhere near them after an accident or quarrel. It is really just a hallucination."

"That is exactly what I thought," the Duke agreed with some satisfaction. "I hope therefore you will be able to persuade him that his wound has come from the French guns and has nothing to do with the female sex."

Shenda laughed as it sounded rather funny and then she asked him in a different tone,

"Is he very badly wounded?"

"He was hit in the shoulder and, of course, as it was not attended to immediately on the battlefield, his wound was very painful and septic by the time he could reach the Military Hospital and receive proper attention.

"But I can certainly assure you that Captain Worth

was exceedingly brave and I have recommended him for a medal – which I will make certain he is awarded."

Shenda drew in her breath.

It seemed to be very exciting to be asked to treat a hero of the Battle of Waterloo.

As they drove on, she remarked,

"It must have been very upsetting for you to lose so many men even though you were the victor, Your Grace."

The Duke turned to look at her.

"I only pray that we never have to go to war again. Any man who saw those young bodies lying about after the battle was over and the terrible slaughter of horses would do everything in his power to prevent *any* war."

There was a tone of pain in his voice that Shenda found very moving and she added quickly,

"Now you have really defeated Napoleon my father believed it would mean peace for at least fifty years."

"I am sure your father was right and I will certainly pray that it may be extended to at least a hundred years."

As he was speaking their carriage was climbing up the road that led into the *Faubourg St. Honoré*.

They came to a halt outside an impressive mansion and she thought, although it would be a mistake to say so, that Captain Worth must be a rich man.

The door was opened by a butler who bowed to the Duke.

"I am afraid, Your Grace, that the Captain is asleep at the moment."

"I thought that he would be at this hour," the Duke replied, "so I would like to speak to Higgins."

The butler showed them into a room that was very expensively furnished, although Shenda thought it needed a female touch as there were no flowers and everything in it seemed too formally arranged as if it was seldom used.

The Duke walked to stand in front of the fireplace.

She was just about to ask him some more questions when the door opened and a man came in.

As he advanced towards them, the Duke asked him,

"Good morning, Higgins, how is your patient?"

"He's 'ad a bad night, Your Grace, tossin' about he were and I 'ad to give him some of that medicine you don't approve of what knocks him out."

"I have told you not to give it to him too often," the Duke said. "I dislike anyone feeling pain, but at the same time I think the drugs the doctors supply to those who can afford them are often a grave mistake."

"I agree with you," Shenda came in. "My mother was very much against any form of sleeping pill and when she became ill, she refused to take them even though the doctors tried to press them on her."

"They do so if the patient is at all troublesome and I have told Higgins, who looks after his Master admirably, that he is to avoid using those drugs unless it is absolutely essential."

"I've followed your instructions, Your Grace, but his shoulder be ever so painful after it's been bandaged that I thinks, although it ain't for me to interfere like, that what them doctors put on it stings it rather than 'eals it."

"I would not be surprised, Higgins, but I am hoping this lady I have brought you to look after the Captain will be able to help his shoulder to heal fully without too much further assistance from the French doctors."

The way he spoke told Shenda that he had no use for any doctor.

She remembered reading a newspaper report,

"*Many of the wounded being treated in hospitals in France are worse when they come out than when they went in.*"

"Now what I want you to do, Higgins, is to let Miss Linbury, who is the daughter of a friend of mine and who I am sure is most competent, do what she thinks best for the Captain. I was not at all happy the last time I called to see that he was not improving as he should be."

"I agrees with Your Grace, but as I don't speak the language them doctors speak, I just can't tell them what I thinks."

"I am sure Miss Linbury will be able to do so –"

As he spoke he looked questioningly at Shenda and she responded,

"I speak French quite fluently, Your Grace, and I am sure that you are right in thinking it is a great mistake to drug a patient into insensibility too often."

The Duke gave a sigh of relief.

"Then I can now leave the Captain in your capable hands and I will be interested to hear how he progresses. I am sure that Higgins will look after you too."

He turned to Higgins,

"Miss Linbury's luggage is in the carriage, will you have it taken up to the best room available?"

"At once, Your Grace."

He left the room closing the door behind him.

Shenda realised that the Duke had dismissed him so that he could speak to her privately.

"I am hoping that you will not find it too difficult here. You are very young, Miss Linbury, but I suggest you make it clear from the beginning that are in charge."

"I am sure that as you have brought me here, they will accept me, but I am only afraid of disappointing you."

"I have a feeling and it is a strong one, that you will not do so, but if things get too difficult and if your patient is truculent, then you know where to find me."

"Thank you so much again, more than I can possibly say, Your Grace, and I will do my very best in every way to make this gentleman better and as quickly as possible."

"You can take your time. I shall always be glad to have him back with me, but I feel it is going to be hard for him to get back to work, so to speak."

"Miracles can and do happen. My mother helped a great number of people who had been given up by doctors simply because she believed so much in natural medicine rather than that manufactured by the medical profession."

"In other words," the Duke smiled, "your mother had a herb garden."

"Naturally, Your Grace."

"And my mother had one too," the Duke admitted.

As he was speaking he was thinking that his mother had not been especially interested in the herb garden, even though it had been flourishing for generations before she had married his father.

But he knew from everything he had already heard that the French doctors were completely determined to use the new synthetic medicines, come what may.

They had been specially produced for the wounded without, he considered, being properly tested before being put on sale, but he did not want to complain too much at this stage in case he frightened off Shenda.

He could not help reflecting that in his usual lucky way he had found exactly the right person for young Ivan to put him back on his feet again.

Especially so that he would be then ready to accept the award he had so deservedly earned on the battlefield by his outstanding bravery in the face of the enemy.

43

"I must now return to my house where there will be people waiting for me and I must not be late for the dinner party I am giving this evening for a very beautiful lady."

To his surprise Shenda laughed and as he looked at her enquiringly, she remarked,

"I am sorry if I may sound rude, but from all I have heard about you, Your Grace, I would be very disappointed if you were not in the company of a beautiful lady when not fighting a battle!"

It was the remark the Duke might have expected from Madame Grassini or from Henriette Wilson, certainly not from anyone as young and as innocent as Shenda.

However, he just laughed and commented,

"I am glad I do not disappoint you! But if you are in any trouble you know where to find me. I feel sure your father will be very pleased that you are safe here and will, I hope, not get into any trouble."

"I can only thank you again and again Your Grace."

They moved into the hall and the Duke took his hat from a footman and Shenda followed him outside.

As he climbed into his open carriage, he raised his hat to her as the horses started off.

She had the sudden feeling she was losing her only friend in Paris as she stood watching the carriage till it was out of sight.

Then Higgins, who had joined her, piped up,

"That be a great man and it'll be somethin' to tell your children when you has them that you've met him and he's 'elped you as he's 'elped so many others."

"You are so right and I will always remember his kindness even if I never see him again."

As she spoke she hoped with great sincerity that she would see him again.

Then Higgins added,

"You'll see him right enough. He be really fond of the young Master, and he's in almost every other day since we've been 'ere."

Shenda felt no one could be kinder than the Duke and as she followed Higgins upstairs, she was praying that she would please him.

And that entailed restoring Captain Ivan Worth to good health.

Higgins led her into what she soon realised was the Master suite.

The bedroom was vast with a huge four-poster bed against one wall where she could see a man asleep.

The damask curtains were tightly drawn across the windows and Higgins without saying anything drew them back.

Now she could see the man lying in the four-poster bed clearly and he was extremely handsome.

Dark hair was brushed back from a square forehead to reveal fine almost classical features.

There was a deep frown between his eyes as if he was suffering pain and she could see that he was heavily bandaged on one shoulder.

Higgins came and stood beside him.

"That there shoulder," he murmured, "ought to be healed by now, but the stuff they're puttin' on it seems to I to make it worse."

"Let me see what it is," asked Shenda.

She was speaking only a little above a whisper and she was well aware, however, that the man she was looking at was in a drugged sleep and would not hear her.

Higgins walked towards a beautifully inlaid chest of drawers that was obviously used as a dressing table.

There was a pair of hairbrushes, a tie box as well as candle and there were numerous bottles and pots.

Shenda guessed that these must have been ordered by the doctors.

She picked up one of the pots and realised it was a grease to be applied to a wound and it smelt of some harsh ingredient that was almost repulsive.

She put it down and took up the others.

Each one was more or less the same.

She was quite certain that even if they cleansed the open wound, the stinging that the greases would cause on bare flesh would be very painful.

She looked from one to the other and then she said to Higgins,

"Would it be possible without waking the Captain for me to see his shoulder?"

"He'll not wake whatever us do to him now. He be out for the count, so to speak, and whatever us says or does he'll not know it."

He walked towards the bed as he spoke and then he undid the bandage that covered the Captain's shoulder.

Although Higgins was fairly gentle, Shenda could not help thinking that she could be more so. If he was fully awake, Higgins' movements would definitely hurt him.

Once the bandage was taken off she was able to see his shoulder and that the wound was still inflamed and red.

But Shenda was sure that as it happened some time ago, it should have subsided by now.

"There, you can see for yourself what them doctors are givin' him ain't no good," volunteered Higgins.

"I do agree with you, Higgins, and what I want you to do now is to go down to the kitchen and ask them if they have any honey."

Higgins stared at her.

"'*Oney*! What do you wants 'oney for?"

"I am going to use it temporarily on that wound and then I want you to find me a great number of natural herbs that I am certain will take the inflammation out of it much more quickly than what is being used at present."

"Did you say 'oney?" Higgins asked again as if he could hardly believe his ears.

"*The very best honey they have* and I will watch our patient while you are fetching it."

Higgins drew in his breath as if he would argue and then without another word he walked to the door.

Shenda sat down on the end of the bed and gazed at the man lying asleep.

There was something overwhelming about him that told her without words that he was suffering intensely.

Yet just not physically – but mentally as well.

She did not know why this thought occurred to her.

Except that she had always believed, although she never talked about it, that she possessed the same gift of intuition as her mother.

It always told her when things were right or wrong – especially if it concerned the health of another person.

Now she was absolutely certain that the Captain's wound was not healing as quickly as it should.

Not only because it was being wrongly treated by the French doctors, but because something was concerning him inwardly and that meant a wounded mind.

It took a little time for Higgins to produce what she required and bring it back.

He did not tell Shenda that they had laughed in the kitchen when he had asked them for honey.

"If you has to sweeten up the young lady as soon as her arrives with honey," one of the women had chided him, "you must be losin' your touch!"

She had spoken to him in very broken English, but Higgins had understood what she was saying.

" 'Oney be sweet," he answered tartly, "and that's more than you're bein' to I at the moment!"

As he took the honey pot up the stairs to Shenda, he was still wondering what she wanted it for.

He was thinking perhaps she intended to use it to counteract or perhaps just to mitigate the drugs the Captain had taken.

To his great surprise she took the honey from him and very gently smoothed it over the Captain's wound.

Higgins watched her with growing astonishment as she covered all the inflamed flesh with sticky honey.

And then she spread it round the side of the wound rubbing it gently in with her long fingers.

After she had finished with the honey she waited a few moments before she covered the wound.

She laid clean linen carefully on top of it before she bound it again.

Higgins noticed that she bound the bandages firmly and yet not as tightly as those applied by the doctors.

Picking up the honey pot Shenda put it on the chest of drawers.

After a long silence she proposed,

"Can we go somewhere so I can write out a list of my requirements?

Higgins opened a communicating door at the end of the room and she saw it led into a boudoir also beautifully furnished.

Yet there was something rather formal and orderly about the room as if no one relaxed in it.

There was a secretaire near one of the windows and she sat down and started to write out a list.

"I am sure there is a herb shop somewhere near us, Higgins, if not any shop that sells flowers and plants might be able to oblige you. And I am sure you will not get every one of these different herbs, only some of them.

"I beg you, as they are so very important, to ask the shopkeeper to find them for you as soon as he can."

She handed Higgins the long list and he stared at it incredulously.

As if she thought he could not read very easily, she read aloud,

"Down, Daisies, Elmtree, Golden Rod, True-Love, Solomon's Seal, Tansy, Yarrow and Maidenhair leaves."

"I've not 'eard of any of them," Higgins remarked.

"They are particurlarly recommended for wounds by Nicholas Culpepper. He was a very famous astrologer-physician in the seventeenth century."

"I never 'eard of him neither," Higgins exclaimed, this time a little sourly.

"He was well-known in his time and people still read his books and tracts, which you will not be surprised to hear were then all condemned by the medical profession, but they have, however, proved since to be wonderful for everyone who has used them.

"Herbal remedies have the most amazing powers, and I saw my mother cure sick children and older people almost immediately by herbs when the doctors had given up helplessly."

"Well us might as well move with the times," said Higgins. "But this lot seems that strange to I."

"I don't mind betting, Higgins, you will be saying something different in a week's time."

"I'm not riskin' losing a bet like that, miss. I've a feelin' that you knows more than I and you be bettin' on a certainty!"

"Just wait and see and I feel certain that when your Master does wake up, although his head will be aching, his wound will not hurt him as much as it did before you sent him to sleep."

"All right, I believes you," Higgins grunted, "but there be many as wouldn't!"

Shenda laughed.

"I can believe that. But now will you show me my bedroom? And as I might be called on in the night I would like to be as near the patient as possible."

"I was a-thinkin' about that, miss, while you were writin' down them strange things you needs."

"What had you decided?"

"I thinks the best thing is if you be on the other side of this 'ere room. It be part of the Master suite but as there ain't no Mistress at the moment or likely to be, you might as well be in comfort."

"There I am prepared to agree with you, Higgins."

Higgins walked across the room and opened a door that led into a small room that Shenda thought enchanting the moment she saw it.

It was obviously a woman's room and it had been gracefully decorated by its last owner.

The bed was a four-poster and the curtains were of the softest pale muslin to match the eiderdown.

There were pink carpets, pink curtains and on the ceiling was a picture of Venus surrounded by cupids.

This, Shenda decided, was a room designed by its owner for love – no woman could have slept in it without thinking she was being treated like Venus herself.

"I would love this room," she enthused to Higgins. "But is there someone important who should sleep in it?"

"You needn't be frightened of that. I understands the owner of this 'ere house be far away in the country and he's no wish to be anywhere near the war."

"It is a lovely room and I am sure I will be happy here," sighed Shenda.

There was a slight hesitation before Higgins added,

"That's what I hopes you'll be. Yet it be a mistake to count your winnings before you 'as them."

"I do know, Higgins, and please be very kind and bring my trunks upstairs. I will unpack before our patient requires my attention."

She felt he was about to say something and then he deliberately stopped himself.

She knew instinctively that it concerned his Master and after what the Duke had said, although she tried not to think about it, she felt distinctly anxious.

She was more than a little apprehensive that when the Captain did wake, he might say he had no wish for her services.

*

Shenda was having her supper when Higgins came into the dining room.

Before he even spoke she realised exactly what he had come to say.

"I think I should tell you that the Captain be awake. But I thinks, miss, if you'll forgive I for saying so, it'd be a mistake for you to see him just now."

"Why?" Shenda asked him.

" 'Cos he's got an 'eadache and he ain't in the best of tempers."

Shenda was certain that this was due to the drug he was being given and now it was wearing off it made him feel even worse than before he had fallen asleep.

"Is he complaining about his wound?"

"Not right now, but he's real disagreeable about his 'ead and I thinks you should stay 'ere, miss."

Shenda felt that he was right and that it would be a mistake to thrust herself on the Captain when he was upset by the drug he had been given.

"Very well, Higgins, I will do as you tell me. But if he is bad in the night call me, because that is what I am here for."

"And as I wants to keep you 'ere, I'm glad you 'as the good sense to listen to what I says, miss."

Shenda smiled at him.

"I have now finished my supper and I have enjoyed it very much. I think now I will go into the library to find a book to read and then I will go to bed.

"Please promise that if our patient is worse you will tell me. Otherwise I will wait until tomorrow."

"Now that be sensible and I hopes, miss, you sleeps well."

He left the room and Shenda went into the library.

She had guessed that there would be a library in the house and she had not been mistaken, and it was much like the one at home only smaller.

She picked up three interesting books and retired to her bedroom.

Once again she was thrilled by the beauty of it and

then she recalled it communicated with the boudoir that communicated with the Master suite.

She put the three books down beside her bed and then she walked through the boudoir until she reached the communicating door at the far end.

She stood listening intently and she could discern Higgins talking in his gruff rather amusing way.

Then as he finished what he was saying, she heard the deep clear English voice of the Captain.

He was swearing not violently but positively and it was as if somehow every word was relieving the pain in his head.

She listened for two or three minutes, then turned away and returned to her own room.

If he had been in great pain she knew he would not have been able to swear so fluently or so clearly.

Higgins was right – it would be a great mistake for him to see her at this moment.

If in a fury he threw her out tomorrow morning at least she would spend one night in this lovely bedroom.

The whole scenario made her feel as if she was just stepping into a fairy tale.

*

When she awoke in the morning, Shenda could not think for a moment where she was or what had happened.

Then bright sunlight streaming through the curtains shone on the gold mirror by her bed and caught the wings of one of the cupids climbing up it.

She then remembered where she was and why she was here.

She sat up in her bed and looked at the clock beside her – it was nine o'clock.

She had asked before retiring last night if she could be called at eight o'clock.

It was obvious that Higgins had let her sleep as her patient obviously had no immediate need for her.

She jumped out of bed, rang the bell and drew back the curtains.

The elderly housemaid who she had seen for a few moments last night came into the room.

"Monsieur Higgins has requested me to inform you, mademoiselle," she spoke up in French, "that Monsieur le Capitaine had a good night's sleep and he thought that you would not visit him too early."

"I understand, thank you," murmured Shenda.

"*Le petit dejeuner* will be served as soon as you are downstairs, mademoiselle."

Shenda then washed and wondered if this evening she would be able to order a bath for herself.

Then she put on one of her plainest dresses, hoping it would make her look professional and arranged her fair hair neatly but not as elaborately as she usually wore it.

She smiled graciously at her reflection before she walked downstairs for breakfast.

It was a French breakfast of croissants and coffee and she was delighted to see that there was a pot of honey on the table – as if to remind her, she thought, that it was to be eaten and not used otherwise!

She was just finishing a second cup of coffee when Higgins came into the room.

"Good mornin', miss, have you had a good night?"

"Very good, thank you, Higgins, but do I feel rather guilty at being so late and leaving you so much to do."

Higgins laughed.

"I ain't done much I can tell you. I'm not touchin' that there wound now you've put that sticky 'oney all over it. I've no wish to 'ear what his nibs has to say when he sees what it looks like this mornin'!"

"You are quite right and I think it would be wise for me to go in alone and tell him who I am."

"Perhaps it'd be better if I comes along with you. He is never in a good temper first thing in the mornin'."

"I can understand that because he has been sent to sleep by one of those nasty drugs, but if you have not given him another one the effects should be wearing off by now."

"He certainly has a lot to say, miss."

It was quite obvious to Shenda that he was worried in case his Master was rude to her or if he upset her as he had obviously upset his previous nurses.

As she rose from the table, she smiled at Higgins.

"I have to be brave and see the Captain now – and I hope it will not be as bad as you are anticipating."

"All right. All right, miss, you thinks I'm a fusspot, but I wants to have you 'ere 'cos I thinks them doctors be doin' him no good."

"Then I tell you what we'll do, Higgins. I will cope with your Master if you will go now and fetch me the herbs I wrote down last night. It will take you a little time, but I am sure you will find a shop that stocks most of them."

For a moment she thought that Higgins was going to refuse and then he answered,

"All right, but you be 'ere when I comes back."

"I certainly will be."

She ran upstairs at once while Higgins disappeared down the corridor that led to the kitchen.

Only when she reached the Captain's bedroom door did she draw in her breath.

She was praying that the gentleman suffering inside would not be too offensive when he saw her.

Then she opened the door and entered.

Captain Ivan Worth was sitting up in bed with his breakfast tray beside him.

As Shenda walked across the room towards him, he did not look up and she was certain that he thought it was Higgins.

Then as she reached the bed, he saw her for the first time and his eyes widened.

"*Who are you*?" he demanded.

"His Grace the Duke of Wellington brought me to you yesterday. He has asked me to nurse you and to heal the wound you sustained so gallantly at Waterloo."

"The Duke has asked *you* to nurse *me*?" Ivan asked incredulously. "Why should he do that?"

"I have done quite a lot of nursing in England and I think you are not recovering as fast as the Duke expected."

"So he sent you here to me! Well, I wish he would mind his own business! I have sent away two other nurses and I have no intention of having a woman fiddling about with me!"

He spoke harshly and Shenda gave a little gasp.

"Please let me try to help you. I know I can do so as the doctors have been giving you the wrong medicines and treating your wound in the wrong way."

"I am more than ready to believe that," he snapped. "But I don't want any woman in this house, so please thank the Duke and tell him I have no wish for his interference."

He spoke so crossly and firmly that Shenda knew he meant exactly what he said and he was determined to have his own way.

For a few moments she stood looking at him and then she gave what was almost a little cry.

"Please, please," she pleaded, "don't send me away. I have nowhere to go and no money."

Ivan stared at her.

"I presume you can go back to the hospital where you came from," he muttered.

"I did not come from a hospital. I have never been in one in my life. I have come from England."

"From England to nurse me! I don't know what on earth you are talking about."

"I came to Paris to see the Duke," Shenda told him, "because my father is dead and he sent me to him as I had nowhere else to go and no money."

"What do you mean you have nowhere else to go? You must have relations or friends."

"He sent me to the Duke – because my brother was killed at Waterloo and since the people who worked on our estate had all gone to the war – it had fallen in a bad state and so had our house."

The words came almost brokenly from between her lips and her eyes were filled with tears.

With a tremendous effort she managed to add,

"Papa sent me to the Duke and the only way he felt he could help me was if he put me to nurse you. Please, please let me try. I promise not to do anything to upset you, but I am very sure I can make you much better than you are at present."

"I just cannot see how you can be sure of that, nor is it the Duke's business to send me women he cannot cope with himself."

"He was being kind and he was also very anxious about you," Shenda cried.

"I don't want the Duke or anyone else to mess me around. *And I don't want a woman in this house!*"

Shenda gave a little gasp and the tears ran down her cheeks.

Then Ivan admitted,

"At any rate my wound is better today than it was yesterday, so you can tell the Duke there is no need for any interference on his part."

"It is better than it was yesterday!" she exclaimed. "But do you know why?"

Shenda did not wait for an answer, but carried on,

"It is because I took off the grease the doctors had put on your wound and dressed it with honey. I knew that it would take away the inflammation and, if you leave it, it will take away the pain as well."

Ivan stared at her.

"What on earth are you talking about?" he asked.

"When you were unconscious from a sleeping drug you should never have been given, Higgins took off your bandages and I could see what a terrible state your wound was in. The inflammation was caused by the creams they have given you that I looked at on your chest of drawers.

"So I sent downstairs for honey and although they laughed at the idea, I knew that you would be better this morning."

Ivan put his hand on his bandages as if to see that they were still there and then he mumbled,

"Now I think of it, I recall my mother once saying that honey is a healer – "

"It is a really wonderful healer for you both inside and out. Oh, please – please let me help make you better."

"I have already said I don't want a woman messing me about," Ivan repeated.

However the way he spoke now was very different from the way he had spoken earlier.

"I promise to keep out of sight and out of your way as much as possible – but I swear the honey I will treat you with and the herbs that Higgins has gone to buy will make you feel better in a few weeks if not days."

There was silence for a moment, before he said,

"I suppose I must believe you, but if you annoy me or do anything I dislike, then you must leave at once. Do you understand?"

"Yes, of course, Captain, and I will be sure to keep out of your way as much as I can."

She looked at him and saw that he was scowling, so she added quickly,

"Thank you, Captain, thank you for letting me stay. I really do have nowhere to go and it would be extremely humiliating to have to go back to the Duke again."

Because he did not answer, she added,

"I will wait till Higgins comes back with the herbs I have ordered and then he and I together will attend to your shoulder. Until then I will keep out of sight."

She did not wait for a reply, but hurried across the room and through the communicating door to the boudoir.

Only as she shut the door behind her did she realise that she had been saved.

Saved by no more than the flicker of an eyelid from being sent away.

For a moment she felt almost faint.

It had been, as she was so well aware, a hundred to one chance that the Captain would want to get rid of her and yet now almost by a miracle she was safe.

She could stay as long as he saw as little as possible of her.

'Thank you, God, thank you,' she prayed over and over again as she ran across the room to the window.

As she looked out onto the street outside, she felt as though she had fought a battle on her own.

Although, like the Duke of Wellington at Waterloo the odds had been against her, she had been victorious too!

CHAPTER FOUR

When Shenda left him Ivan had told himself he was a fool.

He had made up his mind to have nothing more to do with women.

Yet here he was giving in feebly to a woman sent to him by the Duke of Wellington.

At the same time he was forced to admit to himself that she had a point in saying that the way the doctors were treating him was disastrous.

By this time he should be feeling much better than he was so far.

Even to think of a woman brought back Helen into his mind.

He felt his fingers clench together as they had done when she first upset him.

Ever since he had left Eton and Oxford he had been pursued by women –

Not only because his father was so immensely rich and had an important title, but also because he himself was exceedingly good-looking.

It was impossible with his background for women not to find him very desirable from a Social point of view, and even more so when they met him.

Even when he was a schoolboy many women had admired him and told his mother how attractive he was and she often said when he was older,

"I hope, darling, that you will marry someone who will love you for yourself, just as I loved your father – and not because you are a friend of the Prince Regent."

When the Prince of Wales became Prince Regent because of his father's illness, he looked to Ivan for help and he was asked to every party at Carlton House.

He was surprisingly knowledgeable about pictures and furniture and the Prince Regent always took him with him when he was searching for new treasures for his house.

He seldom bought anything without consulting Ivan about it even though he was much younger than he was.

"You and I, Ivan, like the same things," His Royal Highness had said a hundred times. "I am not quite certain about a picture I was offered this morning. Come and have a look at it and give me your opinion."

When Ivan claimed that something was a fake, the Prince Regent always trusted him and he took an intense interest in the ornamentation of Carlton House.

It was partly due to this closeness that Ivan did not join a Regiment that was part of Wellington's Army.

The Prince Regent was much against him joining anything which would take him abroad.

In fact Ivan felt that it was his duty to be at home as his father was so ill.

The old Marquis was nearly seventy and his doctors put his ailments down to old age – his son thought it was something more serious than that and yet he did not like to argue with them.

When finally his father suffered a severe stroke and lapsed into unconsciousness, it was indeed impossible for him to go abroad, as he had to take over not only caring for a sick man but his desolate mother as well.

He had to look after an estate that was very short of men and their racehorses needed a great deal of attention.

All these problems increased when his father died and he had to look after all the members of the family – not only those nearest to him but every relation as they now looked to him as the Head of all the Worths.

It was then that Lady Helen Oswald came into his life.

She appeared suddenly in the Social world shining like a bright star and was undoubtedly the most beautiful *debutante* there had been in many years.

She was the daughter of an Earl and so she would naturally have received a great deal of attention as soon as she was presented at Court.

But her outstanding beauty attracted every eligible bachelor in England and she was toasted in the Clubs and acclaimed in all the newspapers.

When Ivan had first set eyes on her, he felt his heart turn several somersaults and there was no doubt that Lady Helen was as attracted to him as he was to her.

It was not difficult for them to see each other and they met every night at the Season's endless parties – and above all at the many extravaganzas hosted by the Prince Regent at Carlton House.

It was at one of the balls when the garden was lit with myriads of fairy lights and Chinese lanterns that Ivan proposed to Helen and she accepted him.

"We must not announce our engagement yet," he insisted, "until I have had a chance of notifying my many relatives. Otherwise they will feel insulted and it would be a mistake to set off on the wrong foot."

Helen had shrugged her shoulders.

"Relations are such a bore," she remarked, "except, of course, we will want their wedding presents."

Ivan had laughed.

"I will give you all the presents you want, but first, my darling, I have to buy you a ring and it will be the most dazzling diamond London has ever seen!"

He thought that no man was luckier than he was.

The next day after he had finished all his duties at Wellington Barracks, he had gone to Bond Street.

He wanted a ring worthy of Helen's beauty, but it was not easy as the shops stocked plenty of rings, but none of them seemed to him fine or unique enough.

He had wondered if the Prince Regent could help him find the ring he required, when unexpectedly Ivan had seen in a pawnbroker's shop a ring that he thought worthy of Helen's lustrous eyes.

It was an emerald and he did not believe, like some people, that emeralds were unlucky.

It was very large in size and was, Ivan thought, an exceptionally beautiful stone, but it had however been put into a somewhat unsuitable setting – perhaps by an Indian jeweller with no idea of taste.

As it was it looked vulgar and even false and then Ivan inspected it more carefully.

He knew the emerald itself was exceptional and one of the finest stones he had ever seen.

He bought it, took it to Bond Street and told them to set it as it should be, but he did not tell Helen about his find.

That evening she enquired delicately,

"When am I going to see the ring you promised me, Ivan, and then we can announce our engagement?"

"Give me two more days," Ivan had answered her. "Then I shall have a surprise for you."

"I am really longing to see it."

That night at the ball they were attending there was a new arrival in London.

It was the young Duke of Sutherland from Scotland and he was, everyone was told, the owner of a vast amount of land and one of the finest castles in the country.

He was handsome and charming and Helen found him to be a good dancer.

Because this particular ball was being given by one of their relatives, Ivan's mother, although still in mourning, made a great effort to be present.

As he loved his mother very much and wanted her to enjoy herself, Ivan spent a great deal of time at her side.

He had actually noticed that Helen seemed to be dancing several times with the young Duke of Sutherland, and as she appeared to be quite happy without his attention, he concentrated on his mother.

The following day he was too busy with his Army duties to call on Helen and it was only after luncheon that he was able to get away from the Officers' Mess.

He then hurried himself over to her parents' house in Berkeley Square – it was just across the Square from the house he owned himself.

He had hoped the engagement ring he had taken so much trouble over would have been ready by now, but he received a message from the shop saying they were putting on the finishing touches and that it would be with him the next morning.

He thought how pleased Helen would be when she opened the velvet-lined box to view her engagement ring.

'Now we can announce our engagement,' reflected Ivan, 'and we will be married inside the month.'

When Ivan reached Helen's home, the butler, who knew him well, wished him good day as he entered and a footman took his top hat and cane.

"Her Ladyship is in the drawing room, my Lord," the butler intoned.

"There is no need to announce me," Ivan responded and ran up the stairs.

He opened the drawing room door – and then as he entered the room, he stood transfixed at what he saw at the far end by the bay window.

Helen's parents entertained frequently in their large drawing room, but there were only two people there now.

As they were standing together by the window, they were silhouetted against the sunshine streaming in.

Ivan saw to his horror that Helen was in the Duke's arms *and he was kissing her.*

For a second he did not move and then feeling rage moving up within him, he walked slowly towards them.

He had almost reached them before they became aware of his presence.

Then Ivan spoke and his voice was like a whiplash,

"What on earth is happening? What the devil are you doing?"

He was addressing the Duke, who had then raised his head, but had not taken his arms from around Helen.

"I am afraid, Kenworth," he crowed, "I have beaten you to the post – and Helen has promised to be *my* wife."

"She can do nothing of the sort," Ivan then retorted furiously. "She is engaged to *me*."

"She has no ring to prove it," answered the Duke.

"If you do not get out of this house immediately," Ivan raged, "I will knock you down."

As he spoke Helen moved forward and put her hand on his shoulders.

"You are not to be angry, Ivan, dear. I am sorry if I have hurt you, but I want to marry Ewen."

"But you are engaged to me, Helen, your ring will be ready tomorrow and we have planned our wedding."

"I am sorry, very sorry, but Ewen has asked me to be his wife and that is what I wish to be."

"All I can say is that I think you are a cheat and a liar!" screamed Ivan. "You told me you loved me and I believed you, but all you are looking for is a top-notch title – and that is all you are getting from Sutherland!"

"Now you are being offensive, Ivan."

"I intend to be. I consider that you have behaved abominably, in fact quite outrageously in letting me think you loved me when all you were doing was trying to grab a title that would impress your friends."

He spoke so scathingly and for a moment his voice seemed to echo round the large room.

Then the Duke came in somewhat uncomfortably,

"That's quite enough, Kenworth. I cannot have you shouting in such a rude manner at my fiancée."

"*Your fiancée*. She was mine until you came along, and, of course, you are just a trifle higher up the Social tree *even* if you are a Scot."

The Duke clenched his fist at this insult and Ivan did the same.

Then Helen stepped between them.

"I will not have you fighting over me. Do go away, Ivan, and try to behave decently like a gentleman over this if you are capable of it!"

"*Decently*! If you call your behaviour decent, I call it low and disgusting and you should be ashamed of yourself."

It was then that Helen lost her temper.

"How dare you be rude to me!" she shouted. "Get out of my house and let me tell you that no girl would want to marry you if it was not for your miserable title."

For a moment they faced each other and then Ivan turned on his heel and stalked out of the room, slamming the door behind him.

He would have left without his hat if a footman had not pressed it into his hand.

Then he reached the street and started to walk back to his own house, realising that Helen had struck a major blow not only at his heart but at his dignity.

All London would be sniggering tonight at the story of how he had been swept out by the Duke.

There were a number of women he had taken little interest in who would be delighted to see him humiliated.

It was then and there that he decided that he would not stop to hear their laughter or their sniggers.

He wrote a note to his Colonel saying he wished to resign from the Regiment because he had decided to leave England to join the Duke of Wellington's Army in France.

"*I can no longer stand aside,*" he wrote, "*while so many men whom I know and admire are facing the greatest menace the world has ever known.*"

Before dark that very evening he and Higgins were aboard his private yacht at the Port of Tilbury.

"From now on I will no longer be using my title," he instructed Higgins. "You will address me as 'sir' and to the world I am merely 'Lieutenant Ivan Worth'."

Because he had known him for some years, Higgins said nothing, but as he was so fond of his Master he had cursed Lady Helen and wished her bad luck.

A short while later the sails went up the masts and the yacht moved out into the English Channel.

Looking back Ivan could remember all too clearly his feelings as they sailed towards the French coast.

The Duke of Wellington had accepted him and he was immediately involved in the preparations for the battle.

Only then did he feel the pain and humiliation of all that had happened to him begin to gradually ebb away.

He told himself, however, that he loathed women – *all women*.

Like Helen they were interested only in what a man could give them, not the man himself.

'I will never love a woman again,' he told himself.

When the fighting in France began, he strongly felt that every Frenchman he shot down represented the woman he desperately wished to erase from his life for ever.

Then he was wounded in the shoulder and finally taken by the Duke of Wellington to Paris and was installed in the comfortable house in the *Faubourg St Honoré*.

There he had hated all the nurses and all the doctors provided for him.

As he was rich he was able to have a nurse on duty during the day and another at night. They were to attend him as if he was someone very precious, which indeed he was as the Duke's protégé.

The difficulty was, however, that the moment the nurses came into his bedroom, he instantly felt aggressive.

It was impossible for him even to look at them and to hear their voices made him think of Helen.

He became so disagreeable that they refused to go on nursing him and when he heard that they had left he was delighted!

Yet he was forced to admit that the doctors made his wound seem even more painful and they were certainly rougher when they bandaged him than the nurses were.

What he wanted above all was to get well.

He was aware, although he hated to admit it, that his shoulder was considerably less painful since it had been treated by this new nurse.

But he did not want to think of her as a woman.

Therefore when she came to treat his arm, he closed his eyes and pretended he was asleep.

*

Shenda was delighted at what Higgins had brought back to her – they were not by any means all the items on her list – yet there were enough to make up her mother's healing cream that had been famous in the village and the County for so many years.

She started to mix the leaves together as the chef regarded her scornfully.

She was not surprised to find that there were only male staff in the kitchen and, with the exception of the two old housemaids, there were no other women in the house.

Some of the leaves were rather dried up and others seemed too small to be useful.

Then she steamed the leaves until they made what the chef thought appeared to be a nasty smelly mess that would not help anyone.

However, Shenda allowed it cool and added just a few berries to it and then the chef had to admit that it smelt better than the horrible grease Higgins had been using on his Master's shoulder.

When Shenda added a little honey, it looked quite palatable.

"Now I have something extra and special to add," she announced in her best French, "which I was terrified would not be available in Paris."

"What is that, mademoiselle?" the chef asked.

"These leaves are from the ancient Maidenhair tree and I know that they will make your Master feel better than he has ever felt."

The chef laughed.

"You can't tell me a few leaves will do that."

"You will be very surprised and if I am right I will expect you to make a delicious cake that will undoubtedly put several inches around my waist, but it will be worth it!"

"That I promise to do, mademoiselle. At the same time I just don't believe those little leaves have any magic about them."

"You wait and see – "

She had almost despaired of finding the leaves of the Maidenhair tree in Paris, as Higgins had told her he had difficulty in finding it as it had a different name in France.

"Ginkgo it be, or somethin' like it," he muttered.

"Oh, that is the Chinese name for it," she cried.

"Well, when I makes such a big fuss, they sends for the manager. He spoke better English than them lot and he understands what I wants."

"Thank Heavens for that!"

The pulp of Maidenhair leaves provided a cure her mother had always believed passionately in and had used dozens of times.

People who were distressed and miserable, perhaps at losing someone they loved, recovered almost overnight.

Again there was a touch of honey to give it a sweet taste, but actually the leaves themselves were small, juicy and had a sweet smell of their own.

It was all prepared and the cream which was to be applied to the Captain's shoulder had set.

Shenda carried her concoctions upstairs and placed them on a table in the passage outside the Master suite.

Then she waited for Higgins to inform her when it would be all right for her to enter the room.

She could hear him talking to the Captain who was answering him in monosyllables.

'He is still feeling sorry for himself,' she thought, 'and this will certainly make a difference, but naturally he will not believe me.'

Finally after she had waited for nearly five minutes, Higgins opened the door.

She entered without speaking as she knew her voice would upset and annoy her patient.

As she approached the bed she saw him shutting his eyes and she knew he was pretending to himself that she was not there.

Very gently she carefully undid the bandages on his shoulder from the night before, and when she had removed the linen over his wound she saw that the inflammation had definitely subsided.

Most of the red burning colour had gone.

She just longed to ask the Captain to look at it and to see what had happened, but she was wise enough not to say anything.

She just cleaned his wound gently with warm water and a soft sponge that Higgins had left for her by the bed.

She did not rub the wound with a towel, but let it dry itself.

Then even more gently she smeared on the herbal cream she had made according to her mother's recipe and carefully bandaged the wound again.

She made her touch exceedingly light as she hoped that the Captain would not even be aware of it.

As she finished and he had not moved or spoken, she said to him very quietly,

"I want you to drink this, Captain, and I do promise you that it will make you feel much better in a few hours."

For the first time he opened his eyes and he did not look at Shenda, but at what she was holding in her hand.

"What is it?" he demanded gruffly.

"It is from the Maidenhair tree," she replied, "and I promise you it will do exactly as I have just told you."

She pressed the glass into his hand.

Ivan moved it slowly and with a distasteful look on his face towards his lips.

Shenda was very certain he had expected it to taste disgusting like all doctor's medicines.

To his surprise, however, the drink was sweetened with honey and it had a slight taste of its own that he did not recognise but seemed quite pleasant.

He drank it all down and then Shenda took the glass from him.

She walked towards the door and opened it.

Higgins was waiting outside and without saying a word he entered the room.

He was expecting his Master to say how much he disliked this woman nursing him and that the drink she had given him was absolutely horrible.

Instead of which Ivan said nothing.

After taking away the basin he had been washed in, Higgins left without speaking and he saw that Shenda was waiting for him at the door into the boudoir.

She beckoned to him and he followed her into the room and looking at him keenly, she said in hushed tones,

"I have an idea – "

"What is it, miss."

"I think it is bad for your Master to lie there alone thinking of all that has upset him."

"How do you know he's a-thinkin' of what's upset him, miss? Who's been talkin'?"

"No one here, but I do know instinctively that he is upset and I believe very unhappy."

"Well, you ain't far wrong there!"

"I thought so and as it is bad for him and prevents him from improving as quickly as he should, I want you to bring a piano upstairs for me."

"*A piano*! I expects you to ask me for many funny things, miss, but not a piano!"

"I am sure that he enjoys music and as I play quite well, I am going to play to him and unless he stops me, he will find it far easier than either talking to you or, as I think he is, drifting back into his past all the time."

"I knows there be a piano downstairs, and I'll get the footmen to bring it up. But I wouldn't say whether the Master'll like it or dislike it. I never knows with him."

"I expect before the war he attended many dances."

"That be true, miss."

"And I expect also he went to *Drury Lane* or to one of the other theatres where there was music, dancing and of course pretty girls to look at."

Higgins laughed.

"That's a bulls eye if ever there was one!"

Shenda laughed too.

"Please go downstairs and bring me the piano, and we will see what music can do. Quite frankly it is bad for him to lie there hating women because one has obviously hurt him and wondering how he can wreak his revenge."

"There's not much chance of that happenin'."

Shenda wondered whether she was undertaking too big an experiment so soon after she had arrived.

However, three footmen and Higgins soon returned carrying a very attractive upright piano and she made them set it down near the communicating door.

"If you wants some music for playin', there's some downstairs in what they calls the music room, but I thinks you'd better choose for yourself what you wants."

"Yes, of course. That's very kind of you, Higgins. What I would like you to do is to go and do something in your Master's room. Then when he hears the music, if he dislikes it or insists I stop, you must come and tell me."

She was thinking that she was experimenting and it might all end in disaster.

He could think that she was taking advantage of her position as a nurse and dismiss her immediately.

At the same time she was certain that it was wrong for him to be so introspective.

Her mother had always believed that for a very sick person music was far better than conversation.

"People sit by sick-beds and talk their heads off," she said. "And that is a mistake. If one is ill one is pleased to see people, but not for them to chitter-chatter for ages."

"How can we show someone we are sorry that they are ill?" Shenda had asked her when she was very young.

"You bring them flowers and you stay only a very short time. Then after you have gone, they can appreciate the flowers and think of the things they might have said to you – but which were much better not said."

Shenda had not understood this advice at the time, but when her grandmother was ill, her mother had insisted on her playing the piano.

She had told the whole family that they were not to chatter by her bedside and her granny loved the music.

Shenda now looked expectantly at the piano which had been put at the other end of the room as she recalled as a little girl playing the first piece of music she had learnt.

The footmen had left and Higgins had gone into the room next door.

She ran her fingers gently over the keys and started to play a soft tune that made her think about the garden and flowers at home.

She continued playing and thinking she was riding through the woods on Samson, and birds were fluttering in the trees and squirrels scampering on the branches.

She was feeling bright sunshine streaming through the leaves.

She reached the pool in the centre of the wood and there was a slight movement on the surface as if the water-nymphs were hiding from her.

She played on and on remembering again what she had thought when she was riding her beloved stallion.

Her father would be waiting for her in their house when she returned and she was reliving hurrying down the corridor to the study where he would find him sitting in his favourite chair.

Then as she opened the door of the study, he would hold out his arms and smile saying,

"Come on my little one, I have something for you to do for me – "

With a sigh Shenda took her hands from the keys.

She had no idea she had been playing for over half-an-hour and then she was aware that Higgins was standing beside her.

She felt for a split second as if she had come back physically through time to face him.

"What has happened?" she managed to ask.

"The Captain now be fast asleep with a smile on his lips."

Shenda eased herself off the piano stool and tiptoed through the communicating door into the Master suite.

Quietly she then walked to the huge four-poster bed and she could see that Higgins was right.

The Captain was indeed smiling.

It was the first time that she had seen him smile and there was no longer a deep frown between his eyes.

'He is very handsome,' she mused to herself, 'and I am so glad I have been able to help him.'

She stood gazing at him for a while and then turned and went back into the boudoir closing the communicating door behind her.

"He looks better already," she murmured.

"I has to 'and it to you, miss, though I finds it 'ard to say you be right and I be wrong."

"I think we are both right in wanting the Captain to recover quickly."

As she spoke she thought that when he did he might want to return to England, and once again she would have to rely on the Duke to find her somewhere to go.

Then she shook herself – there was a great deal to be done before that could happen.

The Captain's wound had only just begun to heal and even the special herbs which Nicholas Culpepper had recommended all those years ago would take time to work.

"I tell you what I would like to do, Higgins. I want to go out and see a little of Paris. It is so exciting for me to be here and I would love more than anything else to walk down by the Seine."

"Well you can't go walkin' alone and that's a fact!"

"Whyever not?" Shenda enquired in surprise.

"It be like this, miss, them Frenchies have an eye for a pretty girl and you be too pretty to be walkin' about alone."

"Oh, it just cannot be true, Higgins! I have always walked about alone at home, although, of course, it was in the country."

"Well, now you be in a town and a town that be full of Frenchies who wouldn't let you get away with it!"

"But I want to go out and see Paris."

Shenda was thinking as she spoke that perhaps she should ask one of the elderly housemaids to go with her, but that would be a nuisance and a bore. They would be so slow and she doubted if they would want to walk as far as the Seine anyway.

"I'll tell you what us'll do, miss. I won't make it uncomfortable for you. I has to stay 'ere and look after the Master, as you knows, but one of them men downstairs be quite a nice lad and he don't talk much, so you won't have to listen to him."

"You mean he would accompany me?"

"Yes, but I'll tell 'im that you wants to be alone and he's to walk well behind you. It's just in case any of them Frenchies comes up to you thinkin' they can have a bit of fun, so to speak, he'll push them off. Do you understand?"

"Yes, I do, Higgins, and thank you very much for thinking of me. It is so kind of you."

"His Grace says I was to keep me eye on you, miss, and that's what I means to do!"

Shenda ran up to her room to fetch a hat. It was too warm for her to need a coat, so she picked up her handbag.

Downstairs she found a young footman waiting for her in the hall and Higgins was there too.

As she appeared he said,

"Pierre 'ere says as he comes up from the country he would like to stretch his legs. He's quite prepared to walk behind you for as long as you wants, miss."

"I will not be away too long. I just want to have a look at the Seine close to, as I have only seen it from the other end of the *Place de la Concorde*."

"Well, don't you be a-fallin' in," Higgins smirked.

"I will try not to and if I do, you will have to come and rescue me!"

"That'll be the day," Higgins retorted, "cos I can't swim!"

Shenda was laughing as she started to walk down the *Faubourg St Honoré*.

She was aware that Pierre was following behind her but she did not look back.

She walked on thinking how beautiful the fountains were with the sunshine shining through the trees.

She could only walk slowly as there were crowds of tourists walking about on the pavements.

Eventually she reached the River Seine and could see boats and barges moving up and down the river.

The scene was just as fascinating as she thought it would be and she noticed some steps leading down to the river below.

She went down them with Pierre right behind her.

Then she found herself level with the Seine and just ahead was a comfortable seat.

She sat down and now she could view the boats as she really wanted to see them and it was very enthralling.

Someone had once said nothing was more romantic than the Seine at night as then there were lights shining on the river both from the banks and the boats and barges.

'I would love to come here at night,' she mused.

She was sure that if she did the seat she was sitting on would be taken by a courting couple.

She was also certain that Higgins would not allow her to come alone.

She was watching a ship filled with what appeared to be huge logs passing and after it there was a boat with a number of children who were obviously on an outing.

It was then that she heard a man hurrying down the steps behind her and he went to the edge of the water just a little way from her.

He stood there for a moment staring at the river.

Then to her surprise he threw something violently into the water.

As he did so he turned and hurried back the way he had come and was almost running up the steps.

For a moment she could not think what on earth he had thrown into the river.

She thought perhaps it was something he disliked in his house or perhaps some old clothes he no longer needed.

Then as she looked she realised what he had thrown into the river was moving.

To her astonishment it was a *dog*.

It was fighting against the strong current and trying to swim back to the shore.

Shenda jumped quickly to her feet as she realised that Pierre had also moved towards the river.

The dog was small, but he was managing to swim bravely towards the bank even though he was being swept down river by the current.

Pierre joined Shenda as they moved along the bank of the river their eyes glued to the dog swimming towards them.

"How could anyone do anything so cruel?" Shenda cried to Pierre in French.

"I expect he thought that the dog would drown. If he'd been an old dog he would have."

Shenda did not answer him – she was watching the small dog struggling nearer and nearer.

She and Pierre were moving along together so that they were keeping level with him.

Shenda was half afraid he was too small to survive and he would perhaps become so exhausted that he would be swept away by the strong current.

After they had moved quite a long way down the river, he reached the side and without being told Pierre bent down and caught hold of the dog by the back of his neck.

He lifted him onto the bank and they both jumped away as the dog shook himself and water flew everywhere.

Only when she could go near him without getting wet did Shenda bend down and pat the little dog gently on the head.

She could see now that he was a small terrier and obviously not very old.

He might even have been a new unwanted addition to a family and that would explain why the Frenchman had been determined to be rid of him.

He seemed to like her patting him and then Pierre took a large handkerchief from his pocket and dried him.

He liked that too.

Looking at him now that he was fairly dry, Shenda realised she had been right.

He was quite a young dog and seemed well-bred.

Pierre wrung out his handkerchief.

"We'll take him home with us," suggested Shenda. "And I think we should drive back, as he has had enough exercise for the moment!"

"I'll call a carriage, mademoiselle," offered Pierre.

He ran ahead of her up the steps and onto the road, hoping an empty fiacre would pass by.

Shenda was patting the dog and talking to him.

"You were brave to swim like you did, little doggy, and it was very clever of you to save yourself. Now I am taking you to a new home where you will be very happy."

The dog seemed to like her talking to him and after a moment he rubbed himself against her leg.

At that moment Pierre stopped an empty fiacre and Shenda picked up the dog and climbed inside.

She placed the dog beside her on the back seat and Pierre sat opposite them.

"I call that a great adventure, Pierre. We went for a walk and came back with a prize dog, which I am sure will be welcomed by everyone in the house."

She knew as she spoke it was what she was hoping, although perhaps the Captain would refuse to keep him.

He might tell her that, as he had no use for women, he had no use for stray dogs either!

'Somehow I must persuade him to let the dog stay,' Shenda thought to herself.

She wondered how best to introduce him cleverly, as the Captain *must* indeed welcome the small terrier as he had not been prepared to welcome her.

CHAPTER FIVE

When they returned, Shenda told Higgins excitedly all that had happened.

He patted the dog and exclaimed,

"Well, there's one thing about him, he's got pluck!"

"That's a good name for him, Higgins! We'll call him *Pluck*."

The little terrier seemed to like his new name and wagged his tail furiously and then Shenda asked,

"What about the Captain?"

Higgins thought for a moment.

"I thinks it'd be a mistake to tell him about the dog right away. We've got to get him used to *you* first, miss."

"Yes, of course, and I am just terrified I will annoy him and he will send me away."

"Just you go on as you are and us'll keep Pluck in the kitchen when he's not with you."

Pluck was a great success with everybody and chef spoilt him with titbits from almost every dish.

Shenda settled down to do exactly as she had done the first day that had proved reasonably successful.

She treated the Captain's wounds first thing in the morning and last thing at night and only Higgins went into the bedroom during the day.

He did, however, make sure that the Captain drank his Maidenhair tonic every day.

Shenda was somewhat worried that if he took it at night it might keep him awake.

"He be more energetic and he's talkin' about gettin' up," Higgins told her two days later.

"That's wonderful news, Higgins! I was certain the Maidenhair would do the trick."

She had expected the Duke of Wellington to call on the Captain and indeed she would have liked to see him herself, but she was told by Higgins that he had departed for Cambrai to organise the Army of Occupation.

"I suppose His Grace'll call in as soon as he comes back," Higgins reflected. "And it'll give him a big surprise when he sees the Captain."

She was fully aware that the Captain's wound was healing in a miraculous fashion and there was little doubt that he was feeling better, eating more and looking happier.

*

It was now the fourth day she had been in the house and Shenda played the piano in the boudoir after attending to the Captain's wounds as she had every day.

She found the piano gave her an enormous amount of pleasure and she really loved composing whatever she was thinking about.

Now the music she was playing was the story of her growing up and of her happiness at being with her parents.

And of the magic she found amongst the flowers in the garden and in the woods.

She put into her tune the rings of mushrooms that appeared under the trees in the early morning that showed her that the fairies had been dancing there at night.

She played how the squirrels carried their nuts up the trees to hide them and how the goblins would work in the roots as she listened to them by putting her ear against the trunks.

She played to the brilliant stars overhead and to the moon creeping up the sky that had always fascinated her.

She played the tunes all the birds sang in the spring and then her feelings as she first saw the Seine and thought how beautiful it was.

The music of the Seine made her think of Pluck and how the brave little dog had swum to safety after his cruel owner had tried to drown him.

Then she played of her delight when she and Pierre had rescued him and how they had brought him home in triumph!

She looked down and became aware that Pluck who always lay at her feet when she was playing was not there.

She was so used to him being with her that it never seemed at all possible that he might run away and then she noticed with a little consternation that the communicating door was more open than she had left it.

She jumped up from the piano and ran to the door.

She peeped into the Master suite to see that Pluck was sitting on the Captain's bed.

He had grown used in the last day or so to jumping onto her bed and this morning he had licked her cheek to wake her up.

Nervously she entered the room and as she neared the bed she saw with considerable relief that the Captain was patting Pluck in front of him.

He had his head on one side as if he was listening to what was being said to him.

Anxiously Shenda drew nearer and as Ivan looked directly at her, he asked,

"Where did this come from?"

"I and Pierre saved his life the day after I arrived."

He looked at her questioningly.

"I wanted to see the Seine – and Higgins would not let me go alone so Pierre followed me just in case someone interfered – with me."

She stumbled over the last words, but she could see by the expression in the Captain's eyes that he understood.

"I longed to see the Seine and when I reached it, I went down the steps to be beside the water."

Ivan did not say anything and yet she knew that he was listening as she continued with her tale,

"While I was sitting there regarding the boats a man came down the steps and threw something into the river. I thought it was an object he wished to be rid of."

"And it turned out to be a dog," Ivan added as if he felt he had to be a part of the story.

"It was *Pluck* and when he started to swim, Pierre and I were scared he would be swept away by the current."

"He is indeed very small and currents in the Seine are, I know, exceptionally strong."

"He somehow managed to reach the bank and then Pierre pulled him out."

"So he is another visitor in this house for us to cope with," Ivan muttered.

Shenda felt that he was being reproachful, so she explained quickly,

"The staff all love him and it was Higgins who said how plucky he was, so we called him 'Pluck'. I am afraid we are spoiling him which is why he was not frightened to come in to you."

"I should be very annoyed if any dog was afraid of me," he grunted.

"I was not certain if you would welcome him and that is why I kept him hidden."

"He has introduced himself quite correctly, and as I happen to be extremely fond of dogs, I hope you will share him with me."

Shenda smiled.

"You know that I am only too willing to do so. But I have a feeling like most sporting terriers he would prefer to be with a man rather than with me."

Ivan laughed and it was the first time she had heard him laugh and it was indeed a cheerful sound.

"I think this calls for a special tune," he suggested. "So I now suggest that you go back to your piano and tell me how pleased you are that Pluck and I are friends."

Shenda stared at him.

"Are you saying, Captain," she asked him in a very small voice, "that you understand what I have been saying to you in music?"

"Of course I understand. You told me all about the beautiful woods you ride in at home and the birds, squirrels and rabbits that have meant something very special to you ever since you were a child."

Shenda drew in her breath.

"How could you really understand – ?"

"I suppose that the answer is very simple – it is just what I feel myself, so naturally when you put it into music it makes me imagine what you are thinking."

Shenda's eyes lit up.

Then she was afraid that he was speaking to her so naturally that she might make a mistake.

She turned and went back to her boudoir.

She sat down at the piano and played a tune which expressed her joy that he had accepted Pluck – and that he was so much better than when she had first arrived.

She was still playing when she heard Higgins say,

"His Grace the Duke, to see you, Captain."

Shenda took her hands off the keys and listened.

"How are you, my boy?" she heard the Duke say as he must have been walking to the bed, "I am sorry I could not visit you before, but, as I expect you know, I have been in Cambrai."

"I have missed you, sir, but thanks to you I am very much better than when you last saw me."

"I understand from Higgins it is due to the nurse I brought you. He could not speak any more highly of Miss Linbury – and looking at you now I feel prepared to offer her my congratulations."

"I am so much better," Ivan admitted, "and it is due entirely to Miss Linbury throwing away all those doctor's rubbishy medicines and preparing natural herbs for me."

"So I have heard from Higgins, and if you ask me he has never been so astonished in his life at the difference they have made to you."

"They have indeed and now more than anything I want to get up which I think and hope I will tomorrow."

"Now take it easy and don't rush your fences, Ivan. Several of my Officers have suffered a relapse from getting up too soon and your wound was a particularly nasty one."

"I can truthfully say I can hardly feel it now, sir. The reason I feel so well is because of a weird concoction made from the leaves of some tree I have never heard of!"

"Well, you and Higgins have told me everything I need to know and when you are feeling fit enough, you can join me at Cambrai, but actually I think you would be wise to return home on leave. I am sure that the Prince Regent is worrying about you!"

Ivan chuckled.

"I expect the truth is he wants my advice on some treasure he has found in a back street and no one will tell him whether it is good or bad."

The Duke smiled.

"Anyway I expect your own family will be looking for you and I wrote to your grandmother last week and told her that you were in safe hands and that I hoped she would see you soon."

"That was very kind of you, sir, she is the one close relative that I have left and I have often reproached myself for not saying goodbye to her before I joined you."

"Hurry up and get well and you can join me again! Although I daresay there are more important things for you to do at home than there are in the Army of Occupation."

The Duke paused for a moment before he added,

"One of my problems is how to keep the men active and stop them from getting into mischief, which invariably happens when soldiers have too little to occupy them."

Ivan did not reply as the Duke patted Pluck.

"This is a good-looking little terrier – and I am sure he would much rather be roaming the countryside than here in a town, even if it is *Gay Paree*."

"I cannot answer that question as I have not seen anything of Paris yet except those French doctors, who are certainly not as good as French food is reputed to be!"

"What you need, my boy, is plenty of good plain food to build you up, but remember my warning – do not go too fast too quickly."

"I will obey your orders, sir!"

Listening intently Shenda was certain that the Duke smiled at him before he walked towards the door.

As he reached it, he turned back,

"By the way I would like to see your nurse, Miss Linbury, before I leave."

"If you go through the door on your right, you will find her at the piano which you must have heard playing as you came in.

"I did wonder who it was – "

The Duke walked to the door and opened it.

Shenda slipped off the piano stool as he closed the door behind him.

"I congratulate you, Miss Linbury. Higgins told me that the Captain was better, but I can see he has entirely changed since I last saw him – and it is all due to you."

"I am most grateful to Your Grace for sending me here."

Then they both instinctively went to the other end of the boudoir just in case they were overhead by the patient.

The sunshine was streaming through the windows and it shone on her beautiful dark hair.

Looking at her the Duke thought that she was very lovely and that no man who saw her even one as prejudiced as Ivan could fail to find her attractive.

"I hope your patient has not been as difficult as we anticipated, Miss Linbury?"

"He actually spoke to me for the first time today when Pluck, who I was hiding from him, ran into the room and jumped up onto his bed."

"An unusual introduction," the Duke reflected, "but obviously a successful one."

"I am hoping so, Your Grace, as Higgins may have told you, his wound has really healed in a most miraculous way. I was incredibly lucky to be able to buy leaves from the Maidenhair tree to give him energy."

"You may not believe it, but I have actually heard of the Maidenhair tree! Surely it comes from China?"

"It is supposed to be the oldest tree in the world and we were fortunate enough to have one at home which Papa had brought back from China when he was a young man. My mother healed a great number of people with it."

"And now you have healed the Captain. So I am very grateful to you and the next time I come I am sure he will be walking about."

"I think so too, Your Grace. Thank you once again for sending me here. Everyone has been *so* kind to me."

"I am glad and if you need me, I will be in Paris for another two weeks or so before I move to Cambrai."

He walked towards the door and when they stepped out onto the landing Shenda went downstairs with him.

Higgins was there waiting in the hall and the Duke nodded to him as he took his hat from one of the footmen.

"You must admit, Higgins, that I sent you the right person at the right moment."

"That's exactly what I say to Your Grace when you arrives," Higgins replied. "Miss Linbury's shown up them Frenchies and I hopes we never has to see them again."

"I only wish she could do the same for all the men who were wounded at Waterloo – "

"Us still needs her 'ere," Higgins said quickly.

"I know," responded the Duke. "So I will not try to take her away. And please keep looking after her as I hear you are doing so well."

Higgins realised without the Duke saying so that he was pleased that he had arranged for Shenda to be escorted whenever she left the house.

He put a golden coin into his hand and the footmen bowed to him as he walked out of the house.

His open carriage was waiting outside and before he stepped into it he turned towards Shenda.

"Do keep up your good work, Miss Linbury. I am so delighted with what I have seen and I am sure your dog is as good a tonic as the Maidenhair tree."

As the Duke drove off, she waved until he was out of sight and then she turned and ran back into the hall.

"Pluck crept into the Captain's room when I was at the piano," she told Higgins, "and jumped straight onto his bed. The Captain patted him and he spoke to me and asked me why Pluck was there."

"That's just what I 'oped would 'appen, miss, and there's nothin' like a dog to make a man feel he should be up walkin' or climbin' mountains if they be available."

Shenda gave a cry of horror.

"The Duke warned him against doing anything too quickly and the Captain must be persuaded to take things easy until he is really himself again."

She ran up the stairs as she finished speaking.

"I'd better see what Pluck is up to or we may be in trouble!"

She was moving so quickly that she did not hear Higgins answer if indeed he made one.

She ran along the corridor to the Master suite, still feeling nervous of the Captain although he had now spoken to her.

She therefore opened the door quietly, half afraid of what she might find.

She walked in to find that Pluck was still lying on the Captain's bed and his hand was moving smoothly over the dog's back.

Although his eyes were closed she knew he was not asleep.

Without saying anything she went into the boudoir and started to play the piano again.

It was a happy tune, one that expressed her feelings better than anything she could possibly say.

She played of how glad she was feeling that Pluck had been accepted as one of the family.

*

Shenda had found the second day after her arrival that there was a garden behind the house.

The garden was not large, but it contained a number of trees and the lawn and the flowerbeds were all tended by a gardener who came in every other day.

She learnt that there had been a grave shortage of workmen during the war and the owners of several of the nearby houses had agreed that one gardener could see to all their gardens.

The Vicomte certainly had exceedingly good taste, not only in the way the house was furnished but also the way the garden was laid out.

He had made the very best of the ground available and the flowers were a delight.

Now, because she had said how much they meant to her, the servants had arranged flowers in all the rooms she was using.

It was a great relief that there was a large garden for Pluck to run in and so Shenda did not have to take him for a walk whenever he wanted to go out.

At the same time she was still anxious to see more of Paris and when the Captain was asleep she went out to see the sights of the City with Pierre in attendance.

She visited the lovely Madeleine Church and said a prayer not only for herself but for the Captain.

She continued to pray for him as she was dressing his wound and she was sure the combination of her prayers and the cream she had made were together invincible.

Nevertheless she could have been extremely lonely as, although the servants were all kind and attentive, what really made her happy was the library.

She found the books exciting and most interesting and she would retire to bed early and read the latest book that had attracted her attention.

She found it hard to stop herself from reading until nearly midnight, but she longed to have someone to discuss the books with.

She thought she must have expressed this feeling in her music, for rather surprisingly the next day the Captain volunteered,

"I hear you are finding the library very interesting. Is there something you could recommend to me?"

"It's such a beautiful library and I am sure there are dozens of books you will find as entrancing as I do. Tell me what particularly interests you, Captain."

"I suppose anything to do with history will be fine, but not about wars like the one I have been fighting in."

"It would be a great mistake for you to read about wars until you have forgotten all about this one. What are your other interests, Captain?"

Thinking of the Prince Regent, he replied,

"I suppose furniture and I must say from the little I have seen of this house it is well furnished and the pictures are impressive. Have you been to the Louvre yet?"

"I thought about it, but I cannot take Pluck in with me. He might be hurt if I left him at home."

Ivan smiled.

"I believe dogs are more demanding than children, but if you cannot visit the Louvre, I am sure there is a book somewhere in the library illustrating its contents."

"Yes, there will be and I will find it for you and any other books on subjects that interest you."

"Then I will leave it to you. So what interests *you*?"

"I have always wanted to travel," Shenda answered. "Preferably to the East. I would love to see India and any of the other Asian countries."

"India is very beautiful. So find me a book on that country and I am sure I can show you something you can transpose into music."

"What a lovely suggestion! Supposing we start an entirely novel idea of selling music to go with every book. Think how interested the bookshops would be!"

Ivan chuckled.

"As you say, it would be a great new idea and one we could perhaps introduce first into England, although I rather suspect the French are more musical than we are."

"Then we must not give them our new idea before we return to England – "

Even as she spoke she thought perhaps she had said the wrong thing.

She saw by the expression in his eyes that when he thought of England, he remembered all that had upset him at home – which, of course, concerned a woman.

Quickly Shenda sprang to her feet.

"I am going off to the library now. Will you keep Pluck with you or shall I take him with me?"

"Walk to the door," he suggested, "and we will see if he follows you – or stays with me."

Shenda did so and when she looked back Pluck had not moved.

She felt maybe the Captain had cheated, because he was still stroking him, but she knew it would be a mistake to say anything.

She left the room and ran downstairs to the library.

It was not difficult to locate a book of illustrations of the treasures of the Louvre and there was another of all the paintings of Michelangelo and the Italian Masters.

In fact there were quite a number of such books and if she looked for any more she would be unable to carry all of them.

She had actually decided it would take more than two journeys when Higgins appeared.

"What's goin' on in 'ere? I finds you in 'ere, miss, when I thinks you was upstairs playin' the piano."

"The Captain has asked me to find him some books to read, but I do think it would be better for him to look at illustrations first and only start to read a book when he is a little stronger."

"I supposes you're right, as I never has time to read a book meself, I'm all for them pictures."

Shenda laughed as she was sure what he was really saying was that he found it difficult to read and therefore avoided doing so whenever he could.

Higgins took a pile of books upstairs to the Master suite and Shenda followed him with the remainder.

When they walked in, they both stood for a moment without moving.

Ivan and Pluck were both fast asleep.

Higgins placed his books gently beside the bed and Shenda did the same with hers.

Pluck was aware they were there, opened one eye but did not move as Ivan's hand was resting on his back.

Shenda and Higgins then tiptoed from the room and into the boudoir.

As they closed the door behind them Higgins said,

"He be looking better than I've ever seen him and if you asks me that there dog will be a real joy to him. He's always loved animals and there's no one who rides a horse as well as the Captain."

"I might have guessed it and I expect he has some very good horses in England."

"I 'opes one day you'll see them, miss."

"I hope so too – "

But there was a note in Higgins's voice that told her it was most unlikely that she would ever see the Captain's horses.

Of course, she was curious to know who had driven him away and made him hate women so overpoweringly.

However, she was not going to ask a servant.

Higgins had volunteered no information as to what had happened and she therefore had no intention of letting him know that she was curious.

Because the Captain was such a good-looking man there must have been many women in his life, just as there were endless women pursuing the Duke of Wellington.

She had thought about it this afternoon as she was talking to him.

It was not only obvious that the Duke's good looks made him so attractive to women – he also had a charm that one was instantly aware of the moment one came into contact with him.

Shenda was almost sure that the Captain had very much the same charm, but it was somewhat undeveloped and therefore not so strong as the Duke's.

She had wondered, when the Duke was leaving, if he was going to visit one of his beautiful women.

She had heard the servants talking about him and, despite being French, they were exceedingly impressed by the way he had beaten Napoleon at the Battle of Waterloo.

And they could not but admire him for his success with all the beauties of Paris, just as he had captivated the beauties in London.

Shenda was aware that the two old housemaids had peeped at the Duke when he arrived and watched him leave from a window in one of the unoccupied bedrooms.

The footmen and the kitchen servants watched him drive away and her French was good enough to understand what the footmen were saying about him.

They were using colloquialisms that were not in the French curriculum she had learnt at school, but there was no mistaking the innuendo behind the words.

Nor the fact that every man in the house, whatever his position, was envious of him.

They asked themselves why the Duke had such an attraction for women and wished they were in his shoes.

'Perhaps one day,' Shenda pondered, 'I will fall in love, but I hope it is not with a man like the Duke, because however hard one tried one could not help being jealous.'

She could imagine nothing could be more upsetting or heartbreaking than to love a man who had a dozen other women fawning on him, flattering him and telling him how irresistible he was.

'I suppose that wherever the Duke goes, he leaves broken hearts behind him.'

She could remember hearing that his marriage was not happy and she then wondered if it was because his wife was jealous, although there might be less obvious reasons that kept him away from Ireland.

'I don't really understand it,' she told herself, 'but when I fall in love I want the man I marry to love me and not be interested in any other woman.'

Then she thought perhaps she was asking too much.

Her father and mother had always been blissfully happy together, but when she thought of other people she had known, they never seemed to be so content.

From what she had heard there were far too many women weeping over losing a man to another woman.

Yet the Captain was different.

He hated women because some woman must have betrayed him and it had made him bitter, cynical and, as far as she was concerned, frightening – simply because he had the power to throw her out just because she was a *woman*.

Yet by the grace of God and the kindness of the Duke of Wellington she had been able to stay.

So far she had not been made to wonder every other minute where she must go next.

But, of course, when the Captain was well and back on his feet, she would have to again ask the Duke to help her and even as she thought about it, she began to pray that it would not happen too soon.

She desperately wanted to stay where she was now.

For the moment it seemed as if the sun was shining and everything was as she wanted it to be and all because a little dog called Pluck had made the Captain speak to her.

Not disagreeably because she was a woman, but as if she was a human being like himself.

As she thought about it she felt it was not just Pluck who had made things so different – it was also her music.

'He could understand all that I was trying to say to him,' she told herself again and again wondrously.

She found it extraordinary and at the same time the sun seemed to be shining.

The menacing shadows had moved away.

*

The next two days made Shenda feel happy as she had not been since her father died.

In the early morning when she had gone nervously to dress the Captain's shoulder, she feared he might have relapsed into gloomy silence.

To her joy he talked to her about the books she had brought to him and he found to his surprise that she knew a great deal about art and artists.

They had a slight argument, the Captain preferring one Master to another who pleased Shenda more.

They had a duel of words about it and yet he had to admit that she had argued plausibly why she considered her choice a finer artist than his.

As she was finishing the bandaging of his shoulder, she saw that he had already taken his Maidenhair drink.

He had then continued to talk to her about art until the sun was high in the sky and Pluck wanted to go for a walk into the garden.

"I must take him out, Captain. He is very good and always asks by standing patiently at the door."

"He has been well-trained and I just cannot imagine anyone wanting to be rid of such an attractive dog."

"We are indeed lucky to have found Pluck. I will come back as soon as I can."

She did not wait for him to reply, but took Pluck to the garden and then hurried back looking forward excitedly to continuing her conversation with the Captain.

She found that he was not in bed, but sitting in the window.

"You are up!" she exclaimed.

"I thinks it's too soon," Higgins muttered as he was tidying the bed, "but when the Captain makes up his mind to do a thing, there be no stoppin' him."

"I am feeling so much better," he sighed as Shenda walked towards him.

"I want to be certain," he continued, "that my legs are still there and I am perfectly comfortable here and, of course, enjoying the fresh air."

"I told you the magic that Maidenhair leaves would weave, and I hope that the Duke calls today and sees you sitting up. He will be so pleased!"

"I daresay we can carry on our discussion without him and I want that book on the Louvre we were looking at last night."

Shenda fetched it off the pile that Higgins had now arranged tidily on one of the bedside tables.

"Please find the illustration of the Venus in Rome that we were talking about last night and we will compare it with this illustration of the Venus de Milo in the Louvre. You will have to admit that you were wrong in thinking the one in Rome is superior to this – "

They were then back arguing again.

She thought that this was far better for him as until now he had lain silent, hating the injuries he had received both physically and emotionally.

As if he read her thoughts, he remarked,

"It is only a question of days now, not weeks before I am up and about and perhaps able to ride again as I am so longing to do."

"You can ride in the *Bois de Boulogne*, which I am told is fashionable again as it was before the war. There are

101

many fashionable ladies in smart carriages driving up and down to be admired by everyone there."

"That is something you will not be able to do, Miss Linbury, as you have to look after me."

"And what am I expected to do while you are riding with so many people admiring you and your horses, as they admire the ladies?" Shenda enquired jokingly.

"I will jump that fence when I come to it!"

Shenda laughed and then asked a little tentatively,

"Are you really thinking of joining the Duke again in the Army of Occupation, Captain?"

As she asked the question, she saw the expression on his face and then she wished she had not said it.

There was silence for a moment before he replied,

"I have not yet made up my mind. Now let's take a look at one of the other books and see if there is a picture to compare with the one in this book."

He turned over the pages and exclaimed,

"Look at that horse! Is there any other artist who can draw a horse as well as Michelangelo?"

"I think the horses painted by Stubbs are as good if not better," Shenda commented rather provocatively.

Then they were arguing again.

Arguing until Shenda threw up her hands.

"All right, Captain, you win, but it's not really fair, because you have actually viewed many more pictures than I have and I am thus at a disadvantage."

"In other words you now capitulate, Miss Linbury, which is exactly as you should do!"

"Because I am a woman?" she blurted out without thinking.

She knew as she said the words that she had made a mistake.

Suddenly there was a cloud in his eyes and then he retorted rather crossly,

"I think the answer is that I am older, wiser and more experienced than you!"

CHAPTER SIX

Two days later Ivan felt strong enough to venture into the garden.

Pluck was close at his heels and jumped for joy just because he was there.

"It is no use thinking that he is my dog any longer," Shenda remarked rather wistfully.

"I think at present we can share him," he replied.

They walked to find a seat under the trees and Ivan sat down on a bench.

"This is a very beautiful garden," he sighed.

"And that surprises you. Why? Because it is in a City?"

"Yes, and also because, as the Vicomte is not here, I rather expected him to economise on extra servants like gardeners. As the Scots would say, 'the French are awful canny about their money'!"

Shenda laughed and then in a more serious tone she reflected,

"We do all need to be, as the war has made so many people who were rich poor and the poor are even worse off than they were previously."

"I know – and when I return home there is so much I shall have to see to."

He did not say any more, but Shenda was curious as to what his home in England was like.

He spoke as if he owned a large estate, but as she knew he disliked answering questions, she was very careful not to ask them.

They talked instead about artists who had excelled at painting flowers and here they had different favourites too, so the duel started once more.

Shenda, however, was very anxious that her patient should not do too much, so when he rose to walk to the end of the garden to look at the Mews, she advised,

"I think it is time to go back to the house, Captain."

"If you are putting me to bed, I am *not* going," he asserted stubbornly.

"I just don't want you to overtire yourself the first day out, but I thought tomorrow we might drive along the bank of the Seine. I want to show you where I found Pluck and see more of the river."

There was silence and Shenda thought that perhaps she was wrong in suggesting an excursion, she should have left it to him to decide what he wanted to do.

As he still did not speak, she added quickly,

"Of course, if you would rather go alone or wish to visit someone, I will wait at the house for your return."

To her surprise he smiled.

"I was not trying to exclude you from tomorrow's entertainment, I was merely wondering if there might be something more enjoyable – to listen to music at the *Opera House* or, as you have mentioned, a visit to the Louvre."

"I am sure that both activities would be too much for you, Captain. Although it is rather like refusing a slice of birthday cake to a child, as your nurse, I feel I must say you are doing too much too soon."

"If I am, it is what I intend to do! So I will tell you later what my plans are for tomorrow."

"Now you have put me in my place," she responded daringly, "for wanting you to suppress your own orders."

"You can always tell me, as you most surely will, with your music. I know the reproachful notes when you play them as well as those that ring out when you think you have won a contest and defeated me!"

Shenda held up her hands in protest.

"I have never done such a thing, Captain, at least I have never meant to, and if I have, you are making it sound much worse than it is!"

Ivan chuckled.

"Because I want to hear you play and not because I am feeling tired, I am now going back to the house. I will go to bed, but if I hear you sounding too triumphant on the piano, I will get up again immediately!"

"I am certain that Higgins by hook or by crook will not allow you to do that."

They were both laughing as they walked towards the house.

He went straight to his bedroom, climbing the stairs rather slowly, as if he was actually more tired than he was prepared to admit.

Shenda then returned to the library to look for more books that she reckoned would interest him.

There were several by artists she knew they would argue about and she found their arguments really exciting.

She was always delighted when she could make a point about an artist and then he strongly disagreed and to keep the argument going she deliberately took an opposite point of view.

She had just put a pile of books on the table to carry upstairs when Higgins appeared.

"There be a gentleman 'ere, miss, who says he be a good friend of that Vicomte and that he always stays 'ere when he comes to Paris."

"Does he want to stay here now, Higgins?"

"He insists on it and it's not for I to agree or refuse, so I says that I'd speak to you."

"Then I will see him."

Shenda put down the books and walked to Higgins.

"He says he be the Comte de Solyne, but I always thinks that most of them over 'ere has a title, and it don't mean the same as 'avin' one in England!"

Shenda smiled, but she did not disagree with him.

Equally she felt rather worried as to whether it was correct for them to have the Vicomte's friends staying in the house, which had been let on the Duke's instructions to the Captain.

The visitor was in the small salon by the front door.

When Shenda entered, she found a smartly dressed gentleman who she thought was getting on for thirty-five.

He rose and Higgins introduced them.

"This 'ere, monsieur, be Miss Linbury who's been lookin' after Captain Worth for whom His Grace the Duke of Wellington's rented this house while he recovers from his wounds."

"I hope you have been successful, mademoiselle," the Comte spoke up, "and as I explained to this man, I have always stayed here when I visit Paris and I know my friend the Vicomte would be distressed if you turned me away."

"How long are you thinking of staying, monsieur?" Shenda asked him.

"I expect to be here only one night," the Comte said loftily. "It may be a little longer if I find a good number of my friends have now returned to Paris."

"Then I am sure under those circumstances we can make you comfortable, monsieur."

The Comte thanked her and she ran upstairs to tell the Captain what had happened.

He was in bed and as usual Pluck was lying on the bed in front of him.

"What has happened?" he asked as she came into the room. "Higgins had just finished getting me into bed when a footman came to say we had a visitor downstairs."

"I have been talking to him," Shenda replied. "He is the Comte de Solyne and is a friend of the Vicomte who owns this house. He says he always stays here when he is in Paris."

"Well, there is no reason why, as I am paying the rent, he can foist himself on us now – "

"It might be for just one night only and I thought it seemed rather rude and unnecessary to make him go to a hotel when there are half a dozen bedrooms empty on this floor alone."

He laughed.

"So you are to be generous at my expense?"

"If he does not stay for dinner, it will not cost you anything, except for clean sheets on the bed."

"I can see you are prepared to argue with me, Miss Linbury. And if you insist on doing so, I prefer to have an argument in music!"

Shenda smiled at him.

"I have come to the conclusion that not only do you listen to me better when I am playing, but that you find me more articulate on the keyboard than I am with words!"

She went through the communicating door of the boudoir as she spoke and had disappeared before he could think of a reply.

She sat down at the piano.

She told him how glad she was he had been able to see the garden for the first time and how she knew that he appreciated the flowers and the trees.

She played for nearly an hour and when she went downstairs for tea in the small salon, there was no sign of the Comte.

After tea she played once again to the Captain and then she inspected his shoulder.

It no longer needed bandaging, but she insisted on rubbing a little cream onto it.

As she did so, she commented,

"Apart from the scar it really is as good as new and you are very very fortunate that, as far as we can ascertain, the shot that wounded you did not break any bones."

"It still feels a little stiff," he murmured. "But it no longer hurts me."

"What is important, Captain, is that you are not too tired after going out and walking in the garden."

"I can honestly say to you that I am no more tired than I have been any other evening."

"Then you must say thank you to the Maidenhair tree, and I am sure that you will be sensible enough to go on taking it every day, even when you are feeling well."

"I most certainly will," he readily agreed, "and when I return home I am going to plant a Maidenhair tree in my own garden."

"I hope you will be able to find one. Do not forget that my father had to go all the way to China to find ours. He always said the tree was reputed to be over two million years old."

"At that rate it will not be too difficult to find one to last me out!"

Then they were both laughing and as Shenda turned towards the door, he added,

"Come and see me after dinner. I found a picture in one of the books you brought me just now that I would like to discuss with you."

"I will look forward to that, but I have a suspicion that when I do come up, I will find you asleep."

"Are you prepared to bet on it?"

"No, I am *not*," replied Shenda. "Because if I do, you will be so determined to win you will deliberately keep yourself awake! As you have had your first exercise today you really must rest."

"I will merely take an extra glass of the Maidenhair concoction, and if I do, there is no doubt I will be awake all night and ready to go dancing!"

"I am not going to listen to you. You are being too cock-a-hoop and don't forget, 'pride comes before a fall'."

"Then I will cap that by saying, 'nothing ventured, nothing gained'!"

"I must get ready for dinner, Captain, and I do not expect Higgins will be long with yours."

She went into the boudoir closing the door behind her, wondering whether in perhaps a day or so the Captain might come downstairs for dinner.

They could have dinner together in the small *salle-à-manger* where she had eaten ever since she arrived.

Because it was something she had done all her life, she changed for dinner, even though she would eat alone and retire to bed afterwards.

But now she would be going in to say goodnight to the Captain after her dinner and he would undoubtedly be awake.

She therefore chose the dress she would wear rather more carefully than she had on other evenings.

It was a very simple gown, but it was one her father had liked.

She knew the pale blue of it matched her eyes and made her skin seem all the more translucent.

She arranged her hair in the way her father always appreciated – it was nothing like so austere as when she was trying to look like a nurse.

As she opened the bedroom door, she saw Higgins coming up the stairs with the Captain's dinner on a tray.

She stood aside so he could pass and as he reached her, he stopped.

"That Comte who's stayin' 'ere, miss, told us only 'alf an hour ago he'd be in for dinner. As the chef feels he must give him two more courses than he usually gives you, it won't be ready for another ten minutes or so."

Shenda felt surprised as she had never expected to dine with the Comte – in fact she had almost forgotten he was staying in the house.

When she walked downstairs to the small salon, he was standing in front of the mantelpiece.

He was dressed in his evening clothes and looked very smart.

As she walked in she felt that he was appraising her with expectant eyes.

When she reached him, he remarked,

"I am delighted to learn from the servant that I will have the company of such a beautiful lady at dinner."

He was speaking in French and Shenda replied to him in the same language.

"I thought, monsieur, as you were only having one night in Paris, you would be dining with your friends."

"That particular friend I came to see, mademoiselle,

is unfortunately dining out, but, as I have already said, I am delighted to enjoy your company instead of eating alone."

He was drinking a glass of champagne and insisted on Shenda joining him.

"I intend to enjoy myself as I always do when I stay here. The Vicomte is very generous and when he knew I was coming to stay with him, he usually arranged a party."

"How very kind of him and I am sorry there is not one available for you tonight."

She was speaking lightly, but the Comte responded in a serious tone,

"How could I ask for anything more enjoyable than to dine with a beautiful lady who looks so like the Goddess of Love?"

Shenda told herself that was the exaggerated way she would expect a Frenchman to talk.

She asked the Comte some questions about himself and learnt that he was married and had two children, but he did not seem to be particularly interested in them.

When they went in to dinner, she asked him more questions.

She learnt that his had been an arranged marriage which had taken place when he was very young.

His wife, she gathered, had brought a large dowry and his château was admired by everyone who visited it.

"Do you often come to Paris?" she asked when the conversation seemed to be flagging a little.

"Before the war I spent more time here than I did at home, and now the hostilities are over I can only pray I can come back to the excitement I could always find in Paris."

He bent towards her.

Then in a low voice he hoped the servants waiting on them could not hear, he added,

"I am always looking out for beautiful women like you."

Shenda stiffened.

"You are most flattering, monsieur," she responded to him in English, "but at my home in England we do not always express our thoughts out loud."

The Frenchman laughed.

"Now you are being coy, mademoiselle, and if you run away from me, I promise you that I will run very fast to prevent you from escaping."

Although he spoke fluent English, Shenda thought that he could not mean literally what he was saying.

She therefore replied in French,

"I am interested in hearing all about your family."

"As they are nearly always with me I certainly have no intention of talking about them now they are not here – besides I want to talk about *you*."

He bent forward again as he uttered the last word.

He would have touched her hand with his if Shenda had not moved hers away quickly.

He was very obviously flirting with her and it was something she had never experienced before, but this was certainly a lesson she would remember.

"I am sure," she said discouragingly, "you say such flattering words to every woman you meet."

"Only the beautiful ones," the Comte replied, "and who could ever be more beautiful than you? I find your English complexion and your blue eyes enchanting. You are actually all I have been seeking for a long time – "

The servants brought in the last course and it was as delicious as all the other courses had been.

There was no doubt that the chef was enjoying the opportunity of showing off his skills.

At last dinner was over and the butler announced that coffee would be served in the salon.

Shenda rose to her feet, expecting the Comte to stay behind as he would have done in England, to drink a glass of port.

Then as he followed her, she recalled that in France it was correct for the gentlemen to leave the room with the ladies.

There was no chance therefore of her slipping away and avoiding him.

The salon looked very pretty in the candlelight and the servants had arranged plenty of flowers to please her.

She drank a cup of coffee, refusing a liqueur, while the Comte accepted a large glass of brandy.

When the servants had left the room, he came to sit down on the sofa beside her.

"I find you so enchanting, mademoiselle. I always thought English girls were plain and gauche. But you, as I have already said, are like the Goddess of Love and that of course is what we must talk about now."

"On the contrary, monsieur, it is a subject I am not interested in. I would rather hear about your château and your collection of pictures."

The Comte laughed.

"You are entrancing and let me tell you, *ma cherie*, you will not be rid of me so easily."

He moved a little closer to her – so she rose before he could prevent her from doing so.

She walked over the room towards the window and pulled back the curtains.

She looked out at the moonlight on the garden and gazed at all the trees, the flowers and the silvery magic that was so entrancing.

The casement window was wide open and she was breathing in the fresh air when the Comte joined her.

"Do you want to go into the garden?" he asked her. "I would love to see you in the moonlight and although I am so content with you as you are now – lovelier than any flower in bloom."

He was speaking in French and Shenda replied,

"You must not embarrass me, monsieur, otherwise I must leave you and retire to bed."

"I beseech you not to leave me, mademoiselle."

"Then if I stay, you must talk about other subjects rather than pay me such compliments. It is often said that English women do not know how to receive compliments, and now I know the reason why."

"Then tell me why – "

"Because the French pay compliments that are too glib and too easy. One knows they cannot be sincere."

"But I assure you mine are sincere, *ma cherie*, you are very lovely and how can I waste this moment when we are alone in a wonderful world of our own and there is no one to interrupt us?"

He moved even closer to her as he was speaking.

Then much to Shenda's relief the door opened and a footman came in to collect the coffee cups.

She closed the window and pulled the curtains and then she walked across the room to sit down – not on the sofa where the Comte could come and sit next to her, but in an armchair.

He had followed her and he was just about to speak when Higgins came into the room.

"I thought that I'd tell you, miss, that the Captain be asleep and I've taken Pluck and put him in your room."

"That is very kind of you, Higgins, I will be retiring shortly and I am pleased to hear that the Captain is asleep."

She thought it was just what she had expected to happen as he had been up for the first time and was tired.

Higgins left them and as the door closed, the Comte suggested,

"Now at last we are alone and there is no reason for any further interruption. Come and sit on the sofa and talk to me about yourself and allow me to tell you how much you attract me and how delicious I find you."

"I have already said the subject is forbidden, in fact I have had a long day and, like my patient, I too am tired."

She rose to her feet as she spoke and added,

"Please forgive me, monsieur, but I am not used to late nights."

"Then of course you must lie down. And you will look, I am quite certain, like Venus with cupids singing all around you of *l'amour*."

Shenda giggled nervously.

"I think it is exceedingly unlikely, but perhaps it is something that will happen in my dreams."

There was an expression in the Comte's eyes that made her feel embarrassed.

"*Bonsoir*, monsieur," she intoned and she sounded rather apprehensive.

He said something in reply, but she did not listen as she hurried across the hall and almost ran up the stairs.

When she reached her own room she saw a servant coming out of the room opposite and she was aware that it was where the Comte would be sleeping.

Hastily in case he followed her she opened the door of her bedroom and then as Pluck jumped off the bed, she was glad to see that he was there waiting for her.

She bent to pat him and he was obviously delighted to see her.

She talked to him as she was undressing and while she was brushing her hair.

Then she blew out the candles on the dressing table, leaving only those by her bedside.

She was just about to get into bed when Pluck gave a growl.

It was a very low growl and when she turned she saw that he was looking at the door.

He growled again and instinctively she was aware that there was someone outside.

Too late she recalled she had not locked her door and in fact she was not certain if she could have done so.

She had noticed that all the bedrooms were empty except for those used by the Captain and herself.

The doors of the bedrooms were all locked from the outside as a prevention against burglars and it also made it easier for the housemaids to enter the rooms for cleaning.

Now she looked towards her door with Pluck still growling and it was then she realised that when she said goodnight to the Comte, he had responded,

"*Au revoir, ma cherie.*"

She had not really listened as she hurried away to be rid of him.

Suddenly she was overcome with panic and without thinking, only determined to be safe, she pulled open the communicating door into the boudoir.

The curtains had not been drawn and there was just enough light coming through the windows for her to find her way across the room to the other side.

Even as she hurried she heard the Comte's voice in her bedroom behind her.

She did not know whether he was calling for her, thinking that she was hiding or swearing because he found the room empty.

She only knew that she must get away from him to safety.

She pulled open the door into the Master suite.

There was a large candelabrum by the bed which lit the whole room.

Instinctively she ran swiftly across the room with Pluck following her.

As she reached the big four-poster bed, she saw the Captain was not asleep but sitting up, propped up against his pillows and there was a book open in front of him.

He looked up at Shenda in surprise.

Then as she knelt down beside him, she managed to stammer breathlessly,

"The Comte – is in my room and I am terrified – so *very* terrified!"

Ivan stared at her, but before he could speak Pluck jumped onto his bed and excitedly tried to lick his face.

He held the dog off and asked,

"Whatever are you saying?"

Even as he spoke through the communicating door came the Comte wearing a colourful dressing gown.

She decided he looked unpleasantly sinister without the finery he had worn for dinner.

"*Où êtes-vous, ma belle?*" he now demanded. "If you hide from me, you can be sure I will find you."

There was a thickness in his voice that she realised had not been there at dinner.

In fact she was sure it was due to the large glass of brandy he had drunk in the salon with his coffee on top of all the wine he had consumed at dinner.

"Where are you?" he asked again as he wandered across the room.

Then he saw Ivan sitting up in his bed with Pluck beside him.

Shenda had slipped further down on the floor until she was almost invisible.

For a moment the two men stared at each other.

Then Ivan exploded in French,

"You have no right to come in here and I order you to leave immediately."

"I am seeking a beautiful woman who has run away from me," the Comte replied. "She is only making me more eager for the chase and I have no intention of losing her."

"I don't know what on earth you are talking about, but if you don't leave this room immediately, I will ring for the servants to throw you out!"

Ivan spoke to him vehemently, but the Comte was not listening and appeared oblivious of his rising anger.

Then suddenly he saw Shenda crouching down on the floor beside the bed.

"Oh, there you are!" he shouted. "Now, *ma chérie*, let me take you back to your room so I can tell you how exciting I find you."

Shenda did not reply.

Now Ivan yelled at him violently,

"Get out of here at once, you drunken swine, and if you don't obey me I will make certain you are carried out!"

As he spoke he pulled open a drawer of the bedside table beside him.

He drew out a revolver and pointed it at the Comte shouting,

"Go – or I will shoot you."

For a moment the Comte was immobile.

"Go! Go or you will be sorry you are hesitating."

He waved the revolver at him.

As if he suddenly understood what was happening, the Comte backed away, turned and made for the door

As if he understood that the man was an intruder, Pluck jumped off the bed and barked furiously at him.

It was then that the Comte seemed almost to throw himself out of the room, slamming the door noisily behind him so that Pluck was left inside still barking.

For a moment neither Ivan nor Shenda moved.

As she tried to stand up but found it difficult to rise, Ivan remarked harshly,

"I suppose it's your fault that he came here. Like all women, whatever a man is like you cannot leave him alone. If you have been frightened, it is what you damned well deserve!"

He spoke to her in a tone of disgust.

"It is not true, I did not – "

"Get out!" he raged. "Get out and stay out! I have no wish to see you again. You are just like all women, all completely and absolutely untrustworthy."

"Oh, please, please let me tell you what – "

"*Get out!* Leave me alone. I was such a fool ever to believe you were different."

The way he spoke to her was so violent that Shenda felt aghast.

With a sob she ran to the communicating door and pushed it open.

Then as she closed it behind her she stood still for a moment, resting her back against it and gasping for breath.

As she did so she could hear the Captain swearing,

"*Damn women, damn, damn, damn them all!*"

His voice seemed to grow louder and stronger with every word.

With a cry that came from the bottom of her heart Shenda ran to her room – and it was just as she had left it, looking exceedingly attractive in the light of the candles.

She flung herself onto the bed, hiding her face in the pillows and burst into tears.

She cried helplessly.

She recognised that she was crying not just because the Captain was angry with her.

But she had lost him and the happiness she had felt with him.

How long she cried she had no idea.

She knew that she could never explain away what had happened – nor would the Captain ever listen to her.

*

A long time later when she could cry no more, she told herself she could not bear to see him again.

Now he hated her, as he had hated all women when she had first arrived at this house.

She climbed off the bed and lit the candles that had blown out and started to pack her clothes.

Her trunk was luckily in the wardrobe room which adjoined the bedroom.

She threw in the gowns from the wardrobe and the more personal things from the drawers. However, she left out the dress she was wearing when she had arrived.

When she finished packing it was still dark outside, so she climbed into bed, but it was impossible to sleep.

She could only think of the fury and contempt in the Captain's voice as he had told her to leave.

She knew that if she could have seen his eyes, they would have shown how much he despised her.

'Just how could he imagine for one moment that I would try to attract a man like the Comte?'

Then she recognised why he was hating her.

Simply because she was a woman!

A woman had once betrayed him so he expected all women to do the same.

It was then that she remembered how different he had become.

When they had been discussing the pictures and the artists who had painted them, no one could have been more interesting or more polite and considerate.

She had been happier with him than she had ever felt in her life.

'*I love him*,' she confessed miserably to herself.

She had not been aware that it was *love* which she had played to him on the piano.

Love that had made her feel that each day was more enthralling than the last.

The hours had seemed golden because she could be with him.

She had at first felt a tenderness towards him as he had been wounded in battle and then because he had been badly treated by the French doctors.

Then she learnt that he had been hurt by a woman.

She longed for him to believe she was different.

It had all happened in such an unusual way and she had not realised exactly what she felt about him.

Now she knew he had captivated her heart from the moment she had first seen him looking so handsome, yet so shattered by the battle.

'I love him, I love him,' she told herself.

She knew that when she left tomorrow morning she would never see him again.

Now she was crying again as she had cried when he had sent her away, shouting at her and hating her because she had reawakened the disgust he had felt for all women.

She had believed that he had found her different and she had discussed so many subjects with him and they had laughed at the same things.

They had battled with words and she really felt that he had accepted her.

He had been injured not only by a French bullet but by a woman he could never forget.

A woman who then personified to him all women, and now she was amongst them.

'I love him, I do love him,' she cried out to herself despondently, 'and I will *never* see him again.'

CHAPTER SEVEN

Shenda waited patiently in her room until she heard Higgins walking along the corridor at a quarter to eight.

She knew that at this time he would wash and shave the Captain before bringing him his breakfast.

She waited very quietly until she heard the door of the Master bedroom click shut.

Then she ran down the stairs.

There were two footmen brushing the hall – one of them was Pierre and she called out to him,

"Please fetch me a fiacre quickly."

He turned obediently to the front door and then she addressed the other footman,

"My two trunks are inside my bedroom, please will bring them down for me."

She knew that the two footmen would not ask any questions, but undoubtedly Higgins would tell the Captain if he realised that she was leaving the house.

Pierre found a fiacre quicker than she expected and her luggage was loaded into it.

She instructed the driver to take her to the Duke of Wellington's house in the *Champs Élysées*.

As the horses started off, she looked back and there were again tears in her eyes as she said goodbye for ever to the place where she had been so happy.

When they reached the Duke's house, she saw there was a carriage waiting outside drawn by four black horses.

She guessed that he must be leaving Paris, perhaps to Cambrai where she knew he would be moving shortly.

She thought she might have to wait and it would be expensive to keep the carriage, so she told the driver to put her trunks down outside the house.

Then she rang the bell and when the door opened she said to the butler,

"I wish to speak to His Grace. Please tell him that Miss Linbury is here."

He seemed surprised that she was calling so early, but he showed her into the salon by the front door.

She only had to wait five minutes before the Duke walked into the salon.

"Miss Linbury!" he cried. "What on earth are you doing here? What has happened?"

"The Captain has sent me away – "

She tried to speak calmly, but her voice broke and there were tears in her eyes.

"I am having my breakfast. Come and sit down and tell me all about it."

The Duke spoke in a calm manner which helped her to bite back her tears.

He took her into the *salle-à-manger* where he was eating alone and ordered Shenda to be brought breakfast.

The man hurried away and the Duke asked,

"Now tell me what has occurred."

Slowly, in a broken voice, Shenda told him how the Vicomte's friend had arrived and how she had thought it right to allow him to stay at least for the night.

When she related to the Duke how he had paid her fulsome compliments, he nodded as if it was to be expected from a Frenchman.

Then she explained how the key of her door had been on the outside and she had not been sensible enough to take it into her room with her.

She could not go on as her tears were choking her.

"I can imagine what happened," the Duke chipped in. "The Comte came into your room."

"I had heard him outside my door – and then ran to the Captain's room – to ask him to save me."

With great difficulty, faltering over every word, she managed to tell the Duke the next part of the story.

How the Captain had driven the Comte out of the room by threatening him with a revolver.

"Good for him! What happened then?"

"The Captain accused me – of encouraging the man and – told me to leave," Shenda faltered.

Now it was impossible for her to say any more and she wiped her eyes copiously with her handkerchief.

The Duke was thinking quickly.

He was about to leave for England and could hardly leave Shenda alone in Paris. But it was too late to find anyone else to look after her.

As she finished wiping away her tears, he said,

"I am going to England because the Prince Regent is giving one of his special parties for me. Thus the only suggestion I can make is that you come with me."

For a moment Shenda could only stare at him.

"Come with – you, Your Grace?" she asked.

The Duke smiled.

"It will doubtless ruin your reputation, but when I reach London I know there are a number of people who will be only too ready, if I ask them, to take care of you."

Then he gave an exclamation,

"I have just remembered that the Earl and Countess of Richmond will be staying with me at Apsley House."

He carried on as if he was thinking aloud,

"Of course, as they are two of my oldest friends the Prince Regent will have invited them and their girls if they are free to his party. So you can stay with me there until we have time to think of somewhere else you can go."

"Are you quite sure I will be welcomed."

"Considering how brilliantly you have cured Ivan, I think there must be many who would welcome you as their nurse! But we will talk more about it later, now do finish your breakfast as I want to be off."

Shenda's breakfast had arrived by this time, but she could only eat a few mouthfuls and drink some coffee.

Then she piped up,

"I am ready now, Your Grace, and are you really sure you do not mind taking me with you?"

"I shall be delighted to have you on the journey."

She knew that the Duke was only being polite, but it somehow made her feel better.

Her luggage was placed on the carriage outside and she jumped in to find herself sitting beside the Duke.

They drove through the *Place de la Concorde* and left Paris with the horses moving at a tremendous pace.

They only stopped for a short time for luncheon at a roadside inn.

However, there was a château waiting for the Duke where they were to stay the night – it was a château that had been taken over by the Army when its owners had fled from the war.

The Duke and Shenda spent a quiet dinner together, and she was glad that he made no mention of the Captain.

Then they both went upstairs to bed.

"I want to leave early, Miss Linbury, and if you are wise you will rest while we are travelling as it is difficult to talk when we are moving at great speed."

Shenda thought he was telling her politely that he did not want her to chatter to him on the way.

The next day she kept quiet and only spoke when he addressed her, as he had a great number of papers with him requiring his attention.

When he was not reading them, he closed his eyes and she felt that he slept a little.

When they reached Calais, Shenda thought she had never travelled so fast before and it was an experience she would always remember.

There was a British warship waiting to transport the Duke to London.

On any other occasion she would have wanted to explore the ship and enjoy being at sea, but she remained alone in a cabin that was surprisingly comfortable.

Yet she could not believe she was leaving France and the Captain behind her and would never see him again.

'I love him, I love him,' she repeated to her pillow brokenly over and over again all through the night.

*

It was not until the early afternoon of the next day that the warship sailed up the Thames and moored on the Embankment.

Thanks to the Duke's superb organisation there was a carriage waiting to take him to Apsley House.

Now that they had actually reached London Shenda was feeling more composed and no longer in tears.

The Duke told her about the Earl and Countess of Richmond who he had said would chaperone her while she was staying with him.

He said he was certain they would help him to find someone to look after her when he returned to France.

"The Richmonds have lately been living in Brussels because at the moment they are hard-up," he told Shenda, "which is not surprising as they have fourteen children!"

"Fourteen!" Shenda exclaimed.

"Yes, indeed, fourteen children and their eldest son, Lord March, fought with me at Waterloo."

He was thinking that their daughter Lady Georgiana had never married, even though she was undoubtedly one of the most acclaimed beauties in London and Brussels.

If he was honest he knew it was because she loved him and in her eyes no man could ever equal him.

This, however, was something he could not say to Shenda and he rather hoped that Georgiana would not be waiting at Apsley House with her parents.

She might be jealous as Shenda had been travelling alone with him and would take a dislike to her.

Shenda, as they drove away from the Embankment, was thinking just how exciting it was to be going to Apsley House.

Of course, she had heard of the Duke's magnificent house and how it was built at the entrance to Hyde Park.

"It is the first house to be seen after passing the toll gates at the top of Knightsbridge," her father had told her. "In fact its popular nickname is *No. 1 London*."

Shenda had expected it to look very impressive and when she arrived at the entrance with its lofty pillars, she thought it really was a fitting background for anyone with so brilliant a career as the Duke of Wellington.

The butler who opened the door bowed respectfully when the Duke appeared and intoned,

"It's delightful to see Your Grace and all London's waiting to greet you now you've come home."

"Only for a short time, I'm afraid, Watkins, but it is nice to be back. Who is here?"

"The Earl and Countess arrived yesterday evening. They expect Lady Jane to join them for the party tomorrow night."

"Anyone else?"

"No, Your Grace."

"Miss Linbury will be staying here, Watkins, so tell the housekeeper to arrange a comfortable bedroom for her and see that her luggage is taken up."

He walked into the drawing room where the Earl and Countess of Richmond were waiting for him.

The Countess gave a cry of delight and held out her arms. He kissed her affectionately, then shook hands with the Earl.

"I see you that have someone with you, Arthur," the Countess questioned before he could explain.

"Let me introduce Miss Shenda Linbury," he said. "She has been in Paris nursing one of my Officers who has been very badly wounded at Waterloo. I expect you knew her father – Lord Linbury."

"Of course I did!" the Countess exclaimed, "and it was very brave of Miss Linbury to go to Paris."

"Linbury left his daughter in my charge," the Duke explained. "But now her patient is well and she is ready to return to London. I want you to help me find somewhere for her to stay."

"There are plenty of rooms with us at the moment,"

the Countess smiled, "as only one of my brood could come to His Royal Highness's party."

"I am going to see him this afternoon, and of course I will arrange that we take Shenda with us when we go to the party tomorrow."

Shenda had not expected this.

"Oh, are you certain, Your Grace" she asked, "that His Royal Highness will not mind?"

"Of course he will not. He was very fond of your father and I am sure he will be delighted to see you."

"Pretty girls are always going to be welcomed at Carlton House," the Earl added, "just as they are here!"

They all laughed and then the Duke said quickly,

"I must go now to Carlton House. When I return I do not mind telling you that both Shenda and I will be very hungry. The food in France was superb, but not so on His Majesty's ship of war!"

The Countess walked to Shenda's side.

"Come with me," she suggested. "We will find out where you are sleeping and we shall then have to plan as to which gown you should wear tomorrow night for the party at Carlton House."

"I am afraid I do not have anything smart," Shenda remarked as they walked up stairs. "I lived in the country with Papa until he died and when I went to France I took only what I thought were sensible dresses with me."

"I can understand, my dear."

"To be completely honest, I don't have anything at all suitable."

The Countess gave an exclamation.

"I think I can help – in fact I am sure I can. I have a dress with me which belongs to one of my daughters and was her wedding gown. I was going to have a little colour added to it as she does not like it being all in white. But it would be a perfect gown for you to wear tomorrow night at Carlton House."

"Are you quite certain that it will be all right for the Duke to ask His Royal Highness for me to be his guest?" Shenda asked nervously.

The Countess smiled.

"As my husband said His Royal Highness is always prepared to welcome a pretty woman, and I am really not flattering you, my dear, when I say you are *very* beautiful, just like your mother, who I remember as being one of the loveliest women I have ever seen."

"Oh, you knew Mama? Please tell me about it."

"Of course I will, but first let us see where you are sleeping."

The housekeeper was waiting for them and Shenda was shown into a very pretty room, not unlike the room she had occupied in France.

The servants brought Shenda a most welcome bath before she dressed for dinner and she enjoyed being able to luxuriate in the hot water and not have to hurry.

The Duke had said he was going to Carlton House to have a word with His Royal Highness and dinner would be served at nine-thirty.

When he returned he was overcome by what he had been told that the Prince Regent had arranged for him.

"He has really gone to town," he told the Earl and Countess. "He is having a special polygonal building put up in the garden – it is a hundred feet in diameter and built with a lead roof. I am not allowed to see the inside until tomorrow night, because it is to be a surprise.

"But I had a glimpse of a covered promenade which

leads to a Corinthian Temple where the guests can admire a marble bust of myself placed on a column!"

"I don't believe it," the Countess laughed.

"It stands in front of a large mirror engraved with a star and the letter '*W*'. I am really quite overcome and feel the best thing I can do is to hide my blushes and not come to the party!"

He was only joking, but the Countess commented,

"You do know nothing amuses His Royal Highness more than an excuse to hold a fête at Carlton House. I do not know if he has told you what he has organised in the Parks."

"In the Parks!"

"In St James's Park there is a Chinese Pagoda and a picturesque yellow bridge ornamented with black lines and a bright blue roof."

"Good Heavens, it doesn't seem possible!"

"And in Green Park," the Earl joined in, "there's a huge embroidery of a Gothic Castle and then in Hyde Park, there are ornamental booths, stalls, arcades, kiosks, swings and roundabouts."

"You are making me more and more embarrassed," the Duke murmured.

But the Countess carried on,

"The trees are all hung with coloured lamps and lanterns are lining Birdcage Walk and The Mall. Railings and low walls have been torn down to widen the entrance."

The Duke held up his hands in horror.

"Five hundred men have been at work for a month, and His Royal Highness is absolutely certain to produce the most brilliant fireworks ever seen in this country."

Shenda was listening to all this attentively and she added excitedly,

"I think the Prince Regent is quite right – after all no one but the Duke could have won the Battle of Waterloo when Napoleon's Army was larger and more experienced than ours."

"That is indeed true," the Earl agreed, "and there is no doubt, Arthur, you deserve every ounce of it."

"You are still making me feel embarrassed – "

"Nonsense!" the Countess exclaimed. "You know you will enjoy being the hero of the evening with everyone telling you how wonderful you are."

"I only hope that is true. Incidentally, His Royal Highness is delighted that we will be bringing Shenda with us. In point of fact he is anxious to see if she is any more beautiful than the other beauties he has invited who from the way he spoke run into thousands!"

They all laughed, but Shenda felt shy.

She had no wish to embarrass the Duke in any way and only hoped that the dress the Countess had promised her was worthy of such an occasion.

She need not have worried.

The next day, after she had slept until it was late in the morning, the Countess brought the gown to her room to see if it fitted her.

It was just a trifle large in the waist, but when she looked at herself in the mirror, Shenda knew that she had never worn anything more becoming – and certainly not more fashionable.

The Richmonds might well be living in Brussels to economise, but where their many children were concerned, it seemed that they were always open-handed.

The gown was from one of the best shops in Bond Street and was made of exquisite French lace and chiffon.

It revealed Shenda's young and perfectly shaped figure and at the same time it flowed out round her feet, making her look almost as if she was walking on the waves of the sea.

In the evening when the Countess came to her room she gave an exclamation of sheer delight as she saw how attractive Shenda appeared.

The Countess herself was certainly dressed for the occasion wearing the Richmond tiara which was very large and glittered with endless diamonds.

She also wore matching necklace and bracelets and she brought Shenda a pretty necklace of pearls which was most suitable for a young girl.

"You are so kind to me," Shenda told her. "I only wish Papa was alive. He would be so pleased to think that I was going to Carlton House."

"I am sure that you will enjoy every moment of the party, my dear, and I myself am curious to see what else the Prince Regent has thought up."

It had been quite impossible all day for Shenda not to think constantly of the Captain.

But when they finally set off for Carlton House, she was too excited to concentrate on anything but the party ahead.

The Duke had told them at luncheon that he had learnt from His Royal Highness that two thousand guests had been invited to be there at nine o'clock promptly.

It was obvious from the congestion of carriages in Pall Mall and the Haymarket that everyone was anxious to arrive early.

The Earl and Countess had intended to be the first guests, but they found a queue in front of them.

As they entered Carlton House they were received by equerries who conducted them to tents and corridors on the front garden.

There the Prince Regent was waiting for them.

He was wearing a Field Marshal's fulldress uniform and Orders from Russia, Prussia and Spain.

He was in very good spirits and greeted the Duke as the hero of the evening with great enthusiasm.

His Royal Highness also said he was delighted to meet Shenda as she curtsied deeply to him.

He told her that he would never forget her father and how brilliantly clever he had been.

Then they moved into the garden and the Duke took them inside the special building to view what he had not been allowed to see the previous night.

The interior was intended to give an impression of summer light, festivity and airiness.

This had been achieved by painting an umbrella-shaped ceiling to look like muslin and decorated with gilt cords.

The whole building was illuminated by twelve huge chandeliers and Shenda could see the Corinthian Temple with the marble bust of the Duke.

They moved down a covered walk hung with vast tapestries entitled *The Overthrow of French Tyranny*, and *Military Glory*.

This all took time and then the Countess suggested,

"Now we should go to the supper tents, which I am told are hung with curtains of Regimental colours printed on silk."

She paused before she added,

"But I think first we might go back to the house as I really want to leave my scarf as it is so hot and to powder my nose."

Shenda laughed.

"I will come with you, Lady Richmond, as I am a little scared of getting lost with so many people moving about."

"I am not surprised, my dear, come along and we will go to one of the bedrooms and then we will rejoin His Royal Highness at the supper table."

"Am I really expected too?" Shenda asked.

"Of course you are. You are with us and we are in Arthur's special party. Therefore we are more important than anyone else!"

Shenda laughed because it all sounded so grand and then she followed the Countess back into the house.

She was anxious to see some of the rooms she had heard so much about and especially she wanted to view the Chinese Room and the Music Room.

As the Countess walked upstairs, she hesitated for a moment before joining her and then she went into a room that she thought might be the Chinese Room.

It was empty – except for one man.

As she looked at him, she gave a little cry.

It was the Captain!

For a moment they just stood staring at each other and then with the words cascading out of her lips, Shenda exclaimed,

"Are you all right, Captain? How could you have come here? Are you quite certain it has not been too much for you?"

Ivan walked across to her, closing the door behind her and turning the key in the lock.

"I sent a servant to inform His Royal Highness that I was here and I was wondering how I could find you.

"*How* could you have left me in that dreadful way without even saying goodbye to me?"

"*You told me to go,*" Shenda murmured.

"I was jealous! Madly and overwhelmingly jealous that you should have been pursued by another man!"

"But he was horrible and beastly," Shenda managed to blurt out, "and I came straight to you for help – as I was so frightened by him."

"And like a stupid fool I sent you away, but surely you must understand I could *not* be without you."

Shenda stared at him.

"What are you – saying?" she asked breathlessly.

"I am telling you that I *need* you more than I have ever needed anyone in my life and I nearly went mad when I realised you had left the house without telling me where you were going."

"You told me – to go, Captain," Shenda repeated.

She found it difficult to speak as she was overcome at finding him here in Carlton House.

And seeing him for the first time dressed in evening clothes looking so smart and so unbelievably handsome.

Everything she wanted to say died on her lips.

"I drove you away," he continued, "because I was mad and crazy. Equally I was hurt and furious that another man should approach you when you were mine."

"*Yours?*" Shenda questioned in a whisper.

"Why are we pretending, my darling? You know that I love you and you told me you loved me."

"*I told you?*" Shenda cried, feeling she could not be hearing right.

Ivan smiled.

"You told me a hundred times in your music! So you can understand that when I found you had gone, I went almost insane."

"But you knew – I would go to the Duke."

"I knew you would go to him, but I had no idea he was travelling to London. So I had to follow you."

"It has not been too much for you?"

"Not now I have found you, my darling Shenda, but I hope never to have to go through such agony again."

"I still – do not understand," she managed to say.

It was then that Ivan moved closer to her and put his arms round her.

"Let me explain a little more simply," he murmured and his lips were on hers.

It was the first kiss Shenda had ever had.

Ivan drew her closer and still closer to him.

His kisses at first were very soft and gentle.

Then his lips became increasingly possessive and more demanding.

She knew that this was all she had ever longed for and what she believed she would never have.

It was love.

The love which moved through her with an ecstasy she could not understand.

As he held her closer still, she felt as if her whole body melted into his.

She was no longer herself but part of him.

Ivan raised his head.

"I love you so much, my beautiful darling Shenda," he sighed. "Now tell me what you feel for me."

"I love you, I adore you," Shenda whispered. "But when you sent me away, I thought that I had lost you for ever – and would never see you again."

"How could you think anything so stupid? Please forgive me, but, as I said, I was madly jealous that another man should even look at you when you were mine."

"I am yours, Ivan. I have cried and cried because I thought you hated me."

"I will tell you exactly what I do think about you."

As he spoke someone rattled the handle of the door and instinctively Shenda moved out of his arms.

Ivan made a sound of impatience and unlocked the door.

Standing outside was the Prince Regent.

"I was told that you were here, Ivan," he trumpeted, "and I am so delighted to see you."

He then glanced over Ivan's shoulder at Shenda and asked with a twist of his lips,

"Am I interrupting something very private?"

"I know that you will understand, sir," Ivan replied, "when I tell you I want to marry Shenda Linbury. When I came here tonight I thought I had lost her for ever and it is something I intend never to do again."

"So you want to marry her!" exclaimed the Prince Regent. "It is something I am delighted to hear, my dear boy. When I learnt that you had run away to fight with the Duke, I was desperately afraid I might lose you."

"I am here, sir, and my wound has been completely healed by the woman I love. I can now only beg you to arrange for our marriage to take place as soon as possible."

The Prince Regent looked at him and smiled,

"Why not *tonight*?" he asked.

"Nothing would suit me better, sir."

"Then all you have to do now is leave it to me! The Archbishop of Canterbury arrived half-an-hour ago!"

He gave a little chuckle and added,

"Always the unexpected, Ivan, that both you and I enjoy. Wait here and lock the door until I return."

He left the room, closing the door behind him.

Ivan put his arms around Shenda again.

"You see, my darling, I am taking no chances."

"Does he really mean, we can be married tonight?"

"There is nothing the Prince Regent enjoys more than a problem he can solve. In this instance it is what I want more than I have ever wanted anything in my life."

"Are you quite sure that I will not make you angry again?"

Ivan laughed.

"My darling, my sweet, believe me, I love you as I have never loved anyone. In fact I did not know about love until you taught me with your music."

"Do you really mean that?"

"I do swear to you on everything I hold sacred that when you played to me, I learnt everything I did not know before about love. The *real* love that I believe you and I have for each other."

"I love you. I do love you so, Ivan. Oh, please go on loving me, as it is so incredibly wonderful, so perfect and everything I thought I would never find."

"It is what we have both found, my adored one."

Then he was kissing her again.

Kissing her until it was quite impossible to think of anything but the wonder and glory of their love.

*

It seemed a long time, but actually it was less than half-an-hour before the Prince Regent returned.

"It is all arranged," he crowed, "and the sooner you are married, the sooner I will be able to sit down to dinner with my guests!"

His eyes were twinkling with anticipation.

"Follow me," he ordered, "but we must avoid the guests who are still arriving, otherwise they will expect me to greet them."

He did not wait for them to reply and Shenda and Ivan followed him down several empty passages.

They eventually reached a small but lovely Chapel at the back of Carlton House.

As they entered they saw the Archbishop arrayed in a brilliant white vestment standing in front of the altar.

At the altar steps was the Duke of Wellington and the Prince Regent called out,

"Arthur will be the Best Man, Ivan, and I will give away the bride."

Ivan walked forward to stand at the Duke's side and the Prince Regent offered Shenda his arm.

Slowly they walked up the aisle.

As they reached the altar the Archbishop started the Marriage Service.

And he performed it with a sincerity that was very moving.

After the Prince Regent had given Shenda away the Duke took off his signet ring and gave it to Ivan.

When he placed it on Shenda's finger, it was a little large for her, but she knew it joined her irrevocably with the man she loved.

As they knelt for the Blessing she was certain that her father and mother were looking down from Heaven and they were delighted that she had found the same love that they had, and was no longer frightened and alone.

It was suddenly very quiet in the Chapel.

Yet Shenda felt that the angels were singing with joy overhead.

When the Marriage Service was completed both the Prince Regent and the Duke kissed her.

Then the host of the evening hurried off to his other guests.

"I expected this to be a very august occasion," the Duke muttered, "but I had no idea that a marriage would take place. I am happier than I can possibly say that you two are joined to each other."

"We will come to see you tomorrow, if we may," said Ivan. "Now I am going to take my wife home."

"God bless you both. I am only sorry that you will not stay for the rest of the evening."

"I think you will have quite enough admirers to tell you how magnificent you are, and how this party is only a very small expression of what the whole of Great Britain feels for you."

"Thank you, Ivan," the Duke replied. "And do look after my protégée. She is a very special young lady."

"I have learnt my lesson, sir. I can assure you I will never lose her again!"

The Duke went off into the garden and Ivan took Shenda back into the hall.

Guests were still arriving in droves, eager to join in the festivities and so they paid little attention to the newly married couple as they slipped out.

By sheer good luck they found that Ivan's carriage was parked not too far from the entrance.

As they drove off, he took Shenda into his arms.

There was no need to say anything.

He kissed her until she felt as if she was floating up into the sky and had joined the angels who had just sung so beautifully at their wedding.

Then as the carriage came to a standstill outside a house in Berkeley Square, Shenda whispered,

"I have no – nightgown with me."

Ivan laughed.

"I doubt if you will need one, my precious. But if it makes you shy, I am sure Higgins will find you something to wear. He has never failed me yet!"

As he spoke they climbed out of the carriage.

To her immense delight Higgins was in the hall and Pluck was with him.

As the dog, barking with excitement, jumped up at her and she bent down to pat him, Ivan suggested,

"You need to congratulate me, Higgins. I have not only found Miss Shenda as I intended to do, but we have just been married. I feel sure that you will provide her with everything she requires until you send for her luggage from Apsley House."

"Leave it to me, my Lord, and may I congratulate your Lordship and your Ladyship on your marriage which will make us, and I speak for all the 'ousehold, extremely 'appy as I believe you'll both be."

Before Ivan could speak Higgins added,

"Anticipatin' that your Lordship'd be successful in your search for Miss Shenda, there be champagne in the boudoir adjoining your Lordship's room upstairs and also some *pâté* sandwiches."

Ivan gave a little laugh.

"You are right in thinking, Higgins, that we did not have time to stay for dinner, so the *pâté* sandwiches will be very welcome."

He took Shenda by the hand and started to climb up the stairs with a happy Pluck following them.

They reached the first landing and there was a door near what Shenda thought must be the Master bedroom at the end of the passage.

When she opened the door, she saw a boudoir filled with flowers and illuminated with candles.

Shenda looked round her somewhat bewildered and then Ivan explained,

"Higgins was certain I would find you tonight when we learnt you had left Paris with the Duke. Equally I was desperately afraid that you might have gone elsewhere and I would have come home without you."

"How could I have known or thought for a moment, my dearest Ivan, that I would find you waiting for me at Carlton House?"

Then she giggled.

"Nor could I have ever imagined when I borrowed this gown from the Countess of Richmond that I would be married in it – *and to you!*"

"You look so much lovelier in it than I could have expected. You are the most beautiful, adorable, wonderful girl in the whole world and I am so proud you are now my wife."

"Oh, please go on thinking that," Shenda sighed.

Ivan poured her a glass of champagne and as she sat down on the sofa, he put the plate of *pâté* sandwiches in front of her.

They were to learn later that the Prince Regent and his guests did not start dinner until after two o'clock in the morning.

"We are going to drink our own health," proposed Ivan. "Two thousand guests are now drinking the Duke's, but no one in the whole party can be as ecstatically happy as I am."

"I pray I will always make you happy. When I was playing to you, I used to pray that you would be happy and stop hating all females."

She said the last words rather tentatively, but Ivan smiled.

"I love you because you are a woman, and because you have taught me the lesson that not all women are as untrustworthy and despicable as I thought they were."

He put his arm tenderly round her as he went on,

"And, my darling, we have a great many things to do together that I think will make us both very happy."

"What sort of things?" Shenda asked. "Does this house really belong to you?"

She thought as she spoke that it could not be, as she had not expected him to own anything that was so large or impressive – undoubtedly a house in such a smart Square in Mayfair could only belong to a rich man.

As if he knew what she was thinking, Ivan replied,

"Yes, it is mine."

Shenda's eyes widened.

"I had no idea. I thought as the Duke was looking after you that you were poor like me."

"As it so happens I am blessed with being very rich and we have a large estate in the country too, my precious, that we must look after together. Before you ask me, I will tell you that there are many well-bred and spirited horses there for you to ride."

"Oh, Ivan, it is all so exciting that I cannot believe it, but how can we possibly have been married in such an extraordinary way? I think I am dreaming – "

"If you are dreaming, then I am dreaming as well. Incidentally, my darling, you are now, because you are my wife, very important Socially."

Shenda looked at him questioningly.

"I did not understand when Higgins called you 'my Lord'. I thought perhaps he was just making everything sound grander."

"You have no idea of my real name?"

Now there was a note in his voice that had not been there before.

"Yes, of course. It is Ivan Worth."

Just for a moment he thought back and heard Lady Helen saying to him caustically, 'no one would ever marry you but for your title.'

He had hoped that Shenda was still not aware who he was, although she might have been suspicious.

Or maybe the Duke might have told her the truth.

Now it dawned on him that what he always wanted and searched for had come true – he had married a woman who had married him for himself alone.

Not for his title that had dazzled every woman he met so that she responded to his position and not to him.

Then as he looked down at the puzzled expression in Shenda's eyes, he sighed,

"My darling, my wonderful little wife, you have not only given me back my belief in myself, but have shown me that not all women are as contemptible as I believed them to be."

"Of course they are not, but I still do not know if you have a different name from the one you used in Paris."

"That is only a part of my name. I am actually the Marquis of Kenworth, and you, my darling wife, are now the Marchioness of Kenworth."

For a moment there was complete silence and then Shenda exploded,

"I don't believe it! Why were you pretending to be just Captain Worth?"

"I was a Captain and very proud of it, but I joined the Duke at Waterloo because I had been disillusioned by a woman and I told him I wanted to be just one of his junior Officers. In fact I wished to be just Lieutenant Worth. But at the Battle of Waterloo I was promoted to Captain. After that you know what happened."

"What happened was that the Maidenhair tree saved you, and please, my darling, the first thing we must do is to try to find a Maidenhair tree to plant in your garden in the country so that it can help other people as it helped you."

"It is truly the *Tree of Love*, my glorious Shenda, and you shall have a hundred if you want them."

He thought as he spoke that he must be the luckiest man in the world.

He knew that Shenda had married him for himself and she was not in the least bit concerned that she was a Marchioness, but with how the wonderful Maidenhair tree had saved him.

'How, just how,' he now asked himself, 'could any woman be more lovable or more perfect in every way?'

He thought that they had won, the two of them, a Battle of Waterloo all of their own.

Like the Duke of Wellington they were completely and absolutely victorious.

*

Much later that night Shenda put her cheek against her husband's shoulder and murmured,

"How can love be so unbelievably thrilling and so wildly exciting?"

"I too find it so utterly different from everything I expected."

"You are not disappointed, my darling Ivan?" she whispered.

"How could I possibly be? I felt that we travelled up into the sky together and the music you were playing for me came from the stars themselves."

"I felt just the same. Oh, darling, we are so lucky, so very, very lucky. How could I have ever hoped when the Duke did not know what to do with me that he would take me to you?"

"He has been our Guardian Angel and at the same time, my precious, you are what I have been looking for ever since I was old enough to become aware of women, yet until I found you I was completely disillusioned."

"All I want, Ivan, is to make you happy. I love you so much that there is nothing in the world to think about or to dream about except for you."

He drew her closer still.

"I love you and I worship you, Shenda. You are so right, my glorious wife, we will now plant our own Tree of Love so that we can make sure that people feel as well and as happy as we do.

"There are thousands of ways we can express our love through helping other people and by banishing from our home anything that is selfish, unkind and hurtful."

He was thinking about Lady Helen as he spoke and then he eliminated her completely from his mind.

He had found the perfect love that all men seek but few are privileged to find.

At this moment it was impossible to feel happier or to be any more grateful to the Great Power above who had brought them together.

Because he seemed reflective Shenda moved a little closer to him.

"I adore you, my Ivan, with all my heart and soul and I hope never to disappoint you in any way?"

"You could never disappoint me. Our wonderful love, my precious beautiful Shenda, will go on increasing year by year until everyone who knows us will realise that is exactly what they are seeking too."

"You say so many marvellous things to me and you must teach me about love because as you realise, I am very ignorant."

"I do not want you to be anything else. The love I have for you, my lovely one, is perfect and never again will I lose you or the love you have given me."

"You really did hear me saying it to you when I was playing the piano?"

"You told me of the love that is truly ethereal and perfect and exactly what I have wanted without realising it ever since I became a man.

"Now, my darling, we can touch the stars together and learn about each other, but nothing we do or think will be more marvellous than what has happened to us tonight."

"I still think I must be dreaming," she whispered. "Please, darling, kiss me and tell me that this is real and I will not wake up."

Ivan laughed very gently.

Then as his kisses became more demanding Shenda felt that once again the angels were singing.

She and he were now moving up into a Heaven of their own.

As Ivan made Shenda his, they both knew that God had blessed them, and would go on blessing them, not only in this life but for all Eternity.